Eleanor's Secret

Brenda W. Craddock

Typeset in Minion Pro

Editing, typesetting and publishing by UK Book Publishing

www.ukbookpublishing.com

ISBN: 978-1-914195-00-6

Author's Note

Newcastle is the town of my birth and growing to adulthood. I love the town, though I now live in County Durham with my husband, a retired Consultant Anaesthetist. He is a great support as are our two daughters, Philippa, and Stephanie who has once again designed the cover of the book. Our grandchildren Annabel and Adam are always interested and encouraging.

With Every Good Wish,
From Brenda
~ Jan 2021

Eleanor's Secret

Chapter 1

E leanor was deep in thought as she walked beside the River Tyne one day in 1890. She was 17 years old and old enough to discern that feeling within her that something was not right. She had never ever questioned her parents' word or authority. She believed in their honesty, their fairness in judgement and their integrity. What she had seen today had shocked her beyond belief and left a big question in her mind. 'Why?'

She and her mother had a good relationship, made even more special in that she was the only daughter with four older brothers. They had always been able to share their thoughts and ideas and opinions on various matters. When she or her mother was unwell, they could always share how they felt and help each other and certainly they could trust one another with confidences. In fact, her mother had recently confided in her that she had not been feeling well for some time and wondered whether she should go to the doctors. Well it was too late now. Eleanor was left wondering if it would have made a difference if she had insisted her mother saw a doctor, but perhaps not, as now she doubted anything could have been done, even if she had seen a doctor.

The reason why she had doubted there was anything serious the matter with her mother was that she was not losing any weight. In fact, her mother complained that she was putting on a few pounds, though she blamed it on her age and said all her friends were gaining a bit of weight. Someone called it 'middle age spread'. Eleanor remembered how her grandmother Nelly had looked before she died. She was so thin and weak that she could barely stand and it was obvious that she was seriously ill. Her mother was not ill, so what had prompted her to do what she did. Eleanor asked herself that question repeatedly. Why had this happened. It did not make any sense.

She had to have time to think and walking beside the river was for her, a good place to think. She did not know what she was going to do. Her instinct was to confront her mother immediately and see what explanation she would give but to be honest she was a little afraid of doing that. She was hopeless with confrontations and never seemed to say the right thing, and somewhere in her thinking was the idea that if she did not talk about it the whole problem would go away. She knew that was really silly but perhaps if she cleared her head with a solitary walk, things would become clearer.

She had inherited her father and mother's love of Newcastle and the great River Tyne, which was not too far from where they had lived when she and her brothers were young. They lived in the area around Sandhill, easily accessed from the riverside and very near to where Eleanor's mother Muriel had been born in 1829. She had actually been born and spent her childhood on one of the oldest streets in Newcastle, called 'The Side' by some people or just 'Side' by others. It was then the main route from the River Tyne to the upper, central part of the town.

Medieval Newcastle had clustered around the river area, near where the Swing Bridge now stood. Muriel often reminisced about the happy memories she had of walking beside the river with her father and exploring the area around it. Even now Muriel often suggested a walk beside the river to her family, although she had not done this recently, which could be an indicator of her not being well. Muriel often told her family, especially when they complained of being bored, that one of her favourite pastimes as a young girl was standing on the quayside watching all the ships and boats which sailed up and down the river. It was always exciting watching the ships as they were loading or unloading the goods they were bringing from or sending to other countries. It was always busy beside the river and there was always something new and interesting to see which made it a good place to spend time, especially if you were bored. 'Bored' was a word their mother disliked and her children knew not to use in her presence.

She had made sure they knew that this great river was very important in the history of Newcastle and had played a major part in its development. This town had grown from very humble beginnings to be a prosperous city, which traded with countries throughout the world.

Eleanor was so deep in thought that she had not realised she was walking with her head bent low and only realised it when a voice said, 'Watch out, you just about knocked me flying.'

'I am so sorry,' Eleanor said, 'I did not see you.' Now that she was looking up, she saw a rather good looking young man and she recognised him as someone whom she had seen browsing among the books in the library on New Bridge Street. It was one of her favourite places. He obviously enjoyed books as much as she did and she wondered if he had noticed her in the library.

Then he said, 'Look I do not know what is bothering you but obviously something is, because there are tears rolling down your cheeks. Why don't we walk along together and if you want to tell me the reason for your tears, you can, but don't worry if it makes you too upset. You know what they say, a trouble shared is a trouble halved and by the way my name is Tom.'

'It was nice of him to be concerned,' Eleanor thought but there was no way she would be sharing her troubles with someone she had only just met. It was her secret and something which would be very difficult to explain, so she would not be sharing it with anyone. She had to work through what had happened by herself and come to terms with it in her own way.

She did not mind Tom joining her, however, so she wiped away her tears and they set off in the direction of the Swing Bridge. When they reached it, they walked to the middle of it and stood looking up and down the river. It was good to stand right in the middle of the river as it were, on this new bridge. It had only recently been opened and was already proving a great asset to the River Tyne.

'Just looking at it,' Tom said, 'you can see that it is different and is quite a feat of engineering. How long did it take to build it I wonder.'

'It took eight years,' Eleanor told him, 'and actually there is quite a story behind this bridge. It is quite unique and my grandfather used to work in the shipyard which was owned by the man who designed this bridge. He is a brilliant engineer whose name will go down in history as one of the great inventors and entrepreneurs of this century. He is an old man of 80 now, and very rich. His name is Lord William Armstrong and in 1872 he retired from all his businesses and I have heard that he spends most of his time at his big country house at Cragside in Northumberland, near Rothbury. It is a beautiful house set on a hillside and surrounded by a great deal of land, which he is planting with trees and bushes to make the property even more beautiful.'

'That is very interesting,' Tom said, 'and by the way what is your name?'

'My name is Eleanor and I have seen you many times in the library. You obviously like books as much as I do.'

'You are right, I do like books, but I have to confess that I have not noticed you Eleanor in the library but that could be, that once I get my head stuck in a book I take no notice of anyone. I must appear very rude at times but fundamentally I am a rather quiet, shy person who is not good at mixing with people. In the library I can have my own space and do what I most like to do, which is read. I am so glad that there is a library in Newcastle, because books are still expensive to buy. It is so good to be able to borrow books because I love reading and get through books quickly. That is why I am a frequent visitor to the library.'

'I agree that we are lucky to have a library because not all towns do and books are such a good tool for learning. I was actually surprised to learn that a resolution to open a library in Newcastle was passed as long ago as 1854 and yet the library was not built in New Bridge Street until 1882 which is quite recent. It is so good being able to borrow books freely because although books are becoming more and more available as this century advances, they are still expensive to buy and completely unaffordable for a lot of people. Our family certainly make good use of the library.'

'What kind of books do you enjoy reading the most, Eleanor?'

'I like history books, probably because my father, who loves history has aroused my interest in it. Both my parents have a particular interest in the history of Newcastle and I have learnt so much about this city especially from my father. In fact I have often said to him that he should write a book about Newcastle. My parents have also ensured that my brothers and I know the history of the River Tyne, because it is such an important river. I have many happy memories of walking with my parents and siblings along the quayside when we were very young. It was one of my favourite family outings. Ships and sailing vessels sailed up and down the river and there was a hustle and bustle about the quayside that we loved and indeed I still do. We are a very close family and loved family outings.'

As she said those words Eleanor could not help thinking if that would still be true when the family heard what their mother had done. It was bound to have an effect on them all. She hoped her mother would tell everyone soon because it was something they should all deal with as a family. It never occurred to Eleanor that her mother would not tell her family and that she would be the only person to know. She did not want to be the keeper of such a secret.

Tom was enjoying Eleanor's company. She was interesting and he felt he would like to know her better. She seemed calmer now and obviously wanted to talk.

'I am very interested Eleanor in what you have been telling me about the Swing Bridge because I do not know a lot about Newcastle. I have only recently come to live in the North. I was born in London and grew up there. It is a great capital city but it is very big and very busy, and to be honest I know very little about life outside London. I thought London was the most important city in the country and it has been quite a revelation for me coming to the North East. I am really enjoying living here.

'The reason for my family being here, is that my father applied for a job with a big shipping company in Newcastle and was successful, so the family moved up here. There are just my parents and myself, I have no brothers or sisters. I wish I had because it is lonely sometimes. I think that is why I like books so much because they are like my friends.

'The only thing I knew about Newcastle when we moved here was what my father told me. He said that it was once ranked as the fourth most important town in England, the others being London, York and Bristol and being a curious sort of chap I have made it my business to find out as much as I can about Newcastle upon Tyne. That is one reason why I spend a lot of time in the library looking for information about it. I know a little but I need to know much more. You said something about this bridge being very important. Why is that, Eleanor?'

'The answer has something to do with its name Swing Bridge, although swing is not truly accurate. I will explain,' Eleanor replied. 'When the bridge was completed in June 1876 it was the largest of its kind ever built and this iron swing bridge with its complex hydraulic machinery was made and fitted by Lord Armstrong's works at Scotswood. My parents took my brother Benjamin and myself down to the river to see the opening of the bridge and you can imagine our disappointment when we were told there was no special opening ceremony despite its uniqueness and as my father would say 'It's genius'.

'We were, however, given a demonstration of its genius. The bridge is able, on a given signal, to rotate, until it is parallel to the river making a clear channel of water to allow ships to sail up to the higher regions of the river To the onlooker it looks as if the bridge is swinging back so you can see how it got its name.'

'Why was it so important to get further up the river?' Tom wanted to know.

Eleanor answered his question.

'Well you see, Tom, there have been bridges over the River Tyne since Roman times and Newcastle hardly existed in those days but since then history has brought dramatic changes and Newcastle's importance as a port for importing and exporting to the whole world has grown considerably. I have to mention here about coal mining because coal is synonymous with the North East and from the beginning of the fourteenth century coal became the town's main export. There was a steadily expanding market for Tyneside coal which shows in these figures. In 1592, 91429 tons of coal were exported from the Tyne and now in the 19th century this had risen to two million tons. Incredible, isn't it?

'You lived in London, Tom and actually London used most of the coal mined in the North East but it was also shipped to other parts of Britain and to European ports.

'This leads me to the other great industry for which the North East is famous and that is ship building. Ships have been built on the Tyne at least since medieval times and the driving force behind the river's ship building industry was the need to transport goods and particularly coal. Shipyards grew up along the River Tyne and large ocean-going sailing ships were eventually built and Newcastle upon Tyne became world famous for ship building using iron and steel There was a huge shipyard higher up the River Tyne at Scotswood where every kind of sailing vessel was built. The shipyards provided work for thousands of people and the huge shipyard at Scotswood was owned by one of Newcastle's greatest pioneers and entrepreneurs, Sir William Armstrong, whom I mentioned earlier.'

'Tell me more about him, Eleanor,' Tom interrupted.

'He was born in Shieldfield, a suburb of Newcastle in 1810, and to please his father trained to be a lawyer but his main interest was mechanics, electronics, inventing and science and he enjoyed inventing and building, and making things with his hands. He was also fascinated with the idea of harnessing water power and he developed a design for an hydraulic crane. In 1845 he converted a crane on the quayside to water power which led to a commission to build hydraulic cranes on Newcastle quayside. In 1847 he left his job as a solicitor to set up a factory at Scotswood/Elswick for the production of his cranes and other hydraulic equipment. This factory was so successful that he extended into arms productivity making naval guns and warships.

'You can probably see the problem now, Tom. There was a big demand from other countries for his naval guns but they were huge and had to be loaded onto very big ships before being transported to the mouth of the River Tyne at Tynemouth. These big ships could not reach Lord Armstrong's shipyard at Elswick because of the old stone arched bridge across the river. The arches were much too low to allow anything to sail through them.

'Lord Armstrong offered to pay for a new bridge but only if the old arched one was demolished. His wish was granted and he built this new bridge, on which we are standing, with hydraulic machinery, enabling the bridge, as I said before, to rotate into a position where it was parallel with the riverside so that the big ships could access his factory. You can see now the importance of this bridge, Tom.'

'Indeed yes. I have really enjoyed your mini history lesson, Eleanor. You did say Lord Armstrong is still alive?'

'Yes, he is ninety now but as I told you earlier he now spends most of his time developing his house and grounds in Northumberland – and another interesting thing about that house is, that it is the first house to be lit by electricity, generated using water power.'

'You are proving to me, Eleanor, that the North-east has a great deal to offer and that is why I will continue to find out as much as I can in the library. I have to say, however, that you seem to have an awful lot of knowledge yourself. I like your mini history lessons. How about you giving me some more of those lessons?'

'I could do that if you really want me to,' Eleanor replied, feeling quite delighted that she had found someone who was so easy to get along with and was interested in books and reading and learning as much as she was. It had saved the day for her.

She was feeling a lot better and felt much more positive that things could be worked out with her mother. Tom had been a welcome distraction from her troubles and she was grateful to him.

'We could meet here tomorrow if you like right here beside this special bridge and I will continue the story of Newcastle. You can ask me as many questions as you like but for now I am going home for my tea. I am very hungry.'

'Good idea,' said Tom pulling her up to her feet from where they were sitting. before setting off in the direction of a café on the quayside.

Chapter 2

They met up again the next morning and Eleanor asked Tom to fire questions at her and she would try to answer them.

'Where did the story of Newcastle begin?'

'Well to answer that question, Tom, I have to go right back in history to the Roman Emperor Hadrian. I am sure you will have heard about him at school.'

Tom nodded.

'Hadrian had a vast Empire which he used to check on from time to time and in 122AD he came to England to check on the Northern regions of his Empire. He was not impressed with the Scots whom he called Barbarians because they were very hostile towards him and so he decided to define the Northern edge of his Empire by building a wall which would separate the Scots or 'Barbarians' as he called them, from England. This wall would stretch from the Solway Firth in the West to Newcastle in the East. It would have to be a very strong wall to keep out invaders, but Emperor Hadrian knew his soldiers well. They were tough, strong men and he knew they could do it and actually it would be good daily discipline for them. In addition it would take their minds off the change of temperature they were experiencing in this foreign land. England is so far away from their homeland of Italy and its hotter climes and they were always grumbling about it.'

'Do you know how long that wall was, Eleanor?'

'The wall was 80 miles long, up to 20 feet high and ten feet wide with mile castles and turret towers along the way, and it would all be built in stone. It was certainly going to be a long laborious task and the wall would end just at the point where we are sitting now, Tom, beside the Swing Bridge. The wall later extended to Wallsend a few miles out of Newcastle and there are no prizes for guessing how that small town got its name.

'There were no bridges over the River Tyne at that time but the Romans decided to build a bridge right where we are sitting at the wall's end. This would be the first bridge over the River Tyne and the reason for it being in this particular place was because it was the lowest practical bridging point on the river. The bridge was called Pons Aelius, in honour of Emperor Hadrian whose family name was Aelius, and Pons of course means bridge. This first bridge was built of wood and raised on stone piers. I find it interesting, Tom that our 'Pons Aelius' bridge is one of only two bridges in the world named after that great Emperor. The second one was built in Rome across one of its main rivers, the River Tiber and it led to Hadrian's mausoleum. I like that link Newcastle has with the world stage as it were, because Hadrian and the Roman Empire had a great part to play in the history of the world.

'The 'Pons Aelius Bridge' lasted long after the Romans left England but eventually became ruinous, until in 1248 a new bridge was constructed called 'The Old Tyne Bridge'. It was in the same place and with the same sound foundations; but by 1362 it was again ruinous and yet another bridge had to be built. It still had the arches but was different in that it had buildings built on it. There were houses and shops, three towers and a chapel dedicated to Thomas the Martyr. In the centre of the bridge was a blue stone which marked the boundary between Newcastle and Gateshead.

'This bridge was also fated because in 1771 there was a great flood in Newcastle which almost destroyed the bridge. The water swept away the middle of the bridge and two of the arches, killing several people, and in the succeeding two days most of the bridge collapsed into the river. A temporary bridge was built and in 1773 work began on a much more permanent bridge, which was opened to the public in 1773. It gave 100 years of service before being replaced by the Swing Bridge.

'Now is that enough information for you today, Tom, or would you like me to continue?'

'I would like you to continue please, Eleanor, but should we make it tomorrow, same place at noon?'

'Great, I will see you tomorrow,' Eleanor said. They set off together to walk up to the town and when they went their separate ways Eleanor felt like skipping home. She had had a lovely day with Tom. She could forget her troubles when she was with him and it was such a relief having something else to think about. She was hoping her mother would speak about recent events very soon. Meanwhile, she was not going to tell anyone. It remained her secret.

She was behaving perfectly naturally at home because if she didn't her mother would sense something was bothering her and ask questions. She wanted her mother to begin the conversation by telling her what she had done but her mother remained silent about it. She managed to talk about other things during that evening meal, and then her mother told her that she had attended a service at St. Matthew's Church which was very close to where they now lived in Summerhill. Eleanor wondered for a moment why her mother had felt the need to go to church, because that was something she did not normally do. Guilty conscience perhaps, but she was probably being silly to be suspicious and resigned herself to reading a book for the rest of the evening. She had to admit that Tom was very much in her thoughts and she could not help wondering what he was doing this evening. Would he be giving her a second thought she wondered. Probably not.

Chapter 3

The next day Eleanor was waiting beside the Swing Bridge at the arranged time when she saw Tom approaching and once again, she thought how good looking he was.

'Hello Eleanor,' Tom greeted her. 'Nice to see you again. I am looking forward to my next mini history lesson' and he sat down next to her.

'The first thing I want you to do, Tom is look up that steep cliff ahead of us. It is a 35ft drop to the river from the top. You can see the old Keep right at the top and that building is all that is left of the old castle. It is the oldest survivor of Medieval Newcastle.

'My talk today is about Castles, Keeps, Gatehouses, in fact all about defence. You will remember I finished yesterday talking about the bridges over the River Tyne and I referred to the Pons Aelius bridge which was the first bridge over the Tyne. The Romans wanted to build a fort to defend the bridge and they were fortunate to have an ideal place to build it at the top of that cliff.

'They went ahead and built their fort and they called it Pons Aelius, the same name as the bridge. A few local people started to settle around the fort perhaps for protection or perhaps with the hope of doing business with the Romans. This could have been the beginning of the township of Newcastle.'

'Was that first fort ever useful to them, Eleanor?'

'Well after the Romans left in 300 AD the region was very vulnerable and was attacked by a number of countries, namely Norway, Northern Germany, Denmark and the Flemish lowlands. The Anglo-Saxon period in the 7th and 8th centuries was particularly bad with terrifying raids by Vikings. The kingdom of Northumbria had been established in the 6th century and the Viking Lords did their best to try and break up the kingdom.

'Next came the Normans, under William the Conqueror, who landed on our shores in 1066. It is strange, Tom, how almost everybody remembers 1066 but knows nothing about the significance of that invasion, to which I will refer soon. England's old enemies the Scots, were still being very troublesome and in 1080AD William the Conqueror sent his eldest son Robert Curthose to lead a military campaign against the Scots. The campaign was successful and on returning to Newcastle defence was still very much on his mind. He looked at the old Roman fort on the top of the very steep cliff promontory and recognised its excellent position from a military point of view. The old Roman Fort built in the 4th century was still in existence but decaying rapidly and he decided to build another fort on the same site but of a much stronger structure. He went ahead with the building of this New Castle and that is where the name of Newcastle originates. This 11th century castle gave Newcastle its name.'

'What did that New Castle look like?' Tom wanted to know.

'It consisted of a wooden tower on top of an earthen mound or motte and it had a moat and bailey, the latter being the open space in front of the castle, usually bounded by a wooden fence or stockade. The castle was in a strong position and was protected well on the North and East and South side and a deep ditch was dug for the defence of the West side.

'The new town of Newcastle was developing and growing quickly by 1134. The old Norman Castle had served its purpose well, but it was falling into ruin and so between 1168 and 1178 King Henry II ordered the castle to be rebuilt in stone and it was a very strong fortress. It took ten years to rebuild at tremendous cost and consisted of a Castle, an imposing Keep, a Gatehouse and a substantial outer Curtain Wall, which kept all the buildings contained. The land within the Curtain Wall became known as the Castle Garth and you can see that Castle Garth today. In fact, it is at the top of the castle stairs, which lead off from The Side and we could go up them when we go home today.'

'I wonder how many people lived in the castle,' Tom queried.

'I do not have an answer for that, Tom. I have never found any information about that at all, but I do know that the castle was lacking in home comforts because in 1247 King Henry added a Great Hall, kitchens and other accommodation within the Castle Garth. Outside the castle walls and in order to further reinforce the least protected part of the castle on the Western side, Henry replaced the former Gatehouse with a much grander and stronger structure sometime between 1247 and 1250. It had two towers with a passage running between them and a vaulted guardroom on either side. This passage provided another way into the castle, but it was well defended with a drawbridge at the front and another at the back. There was also a portcullis which could be raised or lowered to cut off the entrance passage, so that no unwanted visitors could enter, especially the invaders who just might have warfare on their minds.

'As the years went by, there was not so much need for the castle to be defended because protective town walls had been built around the town, and the Gatehouse was neglected and unused.

'Upper floors were added to it in 1618-1619AD when it was converted into a wealthy merchant's house by Alexander Stephenson who rented the building and later it was under the ownership of a London merchant called Patrick Black who lived there with his wife Barbara. There is a story that this Patrick Black may have given his name to the building, as from then on the Gatehouse was known as the Black Gate. At one time there was even a Public House within the building with John Pickells as its landlord and to this day Tom, you can see his name carved into the outer wall of the Gatehouse. I have actually seen it. We can have a look when we go up the castle stairs and through the Castle Garth on our way home tonight.

'Through time small houses began to appear around the foot of the Gatehouse and by the early part of this century the immediate area around the Gatehouse was becoming very neglected. A cluster of small shops grew up there selling second-hand clothes and shoes but it was not long before they were neglected and ruinous. The Gatehouse became like a slum tenement with 60 people living in its passageways between the towers and vaulted guard rooms and in its final days of occupation there were 103 families living in the building in appalling conditions. It attracted unsavoury characters and the whole area around the former Gatehouse was in an appalling condition. It was in grave danger of being demolished in 1840 but the coming of the railways saved it. Between 1847 and 1849 a railway line was built right through the centre of the Castle Garth splitting the Castle Keep and the Black Gate The latter was in danger again in 1856 but the Newcastle Corporation bought the castle and all the buildings within the castle walls and in 1883 the Black Gate was leased to the Society of Antiquaries who over two years restored the Black Gate and converted it into a museum. They cleared the surrounding land and employed John Dobson to do more restoration. It may have been he who added the fourth storey of the Gatehouse with the red tiled roof because that is a much more recent addition.'

Tom interrupted with a comment: 'It is a very strange thing to allow a modern railway line to separate two such historic buildings. Fast trains thundering across that bridge is such a contrast to a medieval building like the Keep.'

Eleanor had something she wanted to share. 'I did hear a silly story about this, Tom. Apparently, an American visitor was heard to say as the train in which she was travelling was passing between the Keep and the Black Gate: "What a pity they built that tall building right next to a railway line."

'Now back to 1400, Tom, when the government of the town of Newcastle changed. Each town in the country had a different way of being governed. Some towns had a sheriff, others had a Lord Mayor or Burgesses or Bailiffs or Guilds and in feudal times every town had a Lord. In other words, there had to be a body of people who controlled the town and kept Law and Order within it. We know for certain that by 1300 Newcastle was governed by a Mayor and four Bailiffs but there was a big change in 1400 when a new charter was granted to Newcastle by King Henry 4th which separated the town but not the castle and its precincts, from the county of Northumberland, and Newcastle became "a county of itself" with the right to have a sheriff of its own instead of the Bailiffs which it currently had. The castle and its precincts continued to be part of Northumberland but the use of the castle as a defence and fortification was declining and it became Northumberland's County Gaol for a short time. Its upkeep was neglected for over 200 years, and it was rapidly becoming a ruin.

'In 1638 the Scots were once again waging war on Newcastle and the castle was partly rebuilt to fend off their attacks. During one of the sieges by the Scots people, Newcastle held out against the Scottish army for three months in the castle and in the Keep for a further two days. The rest of the town's people had already fallen to the Scottish Army. Apparently Charles the 1st who was visiting Newcastle at the time was very impressed with the way the town held out against the Scots. Not a lot of people know that Tom. Everyone knows that Charles the 1st lost his head but the fact that he visited Newcastle during the Civil War and was so impressed with the residents of this town is hardly known at all.'

Once again Tom had a question. 'That old castle served Newcastle well I think but what was its final fate?'

'Well, after the Civil War in the 17th century, there was no further need of the castle as a defence and so it fell into decay once more until 1810, when Newcastle Corporation bought it and built new battlements and replaced the roof to keep out the elements. They even put up a crenelated wall round the top of the Keep to make it look more authentic and put some canons onto the battlements so that they could be fired on special occasions and in festive periods. They restored the Castle Keep and opened it to the public and I remember the Keep from my childhood, Tom. It is something which happened when I was very small. The Newcastle Keep is one of only two Norman keeps in our country which is entered by stairs leading up to its second level and I remember those stairs very well because when I was quite young, about four years of age, my brothers were allowed to take me on an outing to the Keep with strict instructions to look after me very carefully. I only got a few steps up that flight of stairs, holding my brother's hand when I apparently stopped and refused to go any further because my legs were just too tired. I distinctly remember my brothers carrying me up those steps, taking it in turns to do so. Then when we were at the top and I peeped bravely into the entrance, all I could see was blackness and I cried and cried and refused to go in. My brothers were so cross with me as they had to take me home again and to this day they are always reminding me of it.'

'Well that's brothers!' Tom said. 'Why don't you and I visit the Keep together sometime? I think it will be very interesting. It should not be so scary now and I have found out quite a lot about it. You will see that each of the four floors was one big room with a lot of smaller rooms built into the turrets and the walls, because they were so thick. It has a beautiful chapel on the ground floor built into the base of those stairs which lead up to the entrance and which you found so hard to climb when you were small, Eleanor. It must have been dark inside the chapel because there can't have been very much light getting into it. Above the ground floor the Keep is a warren of tunnels, arches and staircases which allow you to climb to the very top and go out onto the roof. There are wonderful views from the top. We must go to the Keep together sometime and see those views. We are going home that way today, aren't we, so we will see if the Keep is open.'

'Yes. I am up for it,' Eleanor said and they set off immediately walking up the Side until they reached the castle stairs which they then climbed to reach the Castle Garth and the Keep. They talked as they walked and had quite a conversation about castles following on from Eleanor's mini lecture.

'It is a shame that the old castle no longer exists, Tom. I wonder what it was like. Big and cold, I should think, like all castles seem to be.'

'Well,' Tom replied, 'castles are notoriously damp and cold even with the great big fireplaces they always have. I would have loved sitting beside one of those enormous fireplaces with the logs burning and crackling and spitting out sparks of soot, though I would not have liked it if one of those hot sparks had fallen on me. Those fires must have been a fire hazard but I suspect visitors to those castles spent a lot of their time getting warm beside them.'

The Keep was open and they were able to spend some time there.

It was very interesting but Eleanor had to hurry away because the family were having a birthday meal for their father's birthday. On her way home Eleanor could not stop smiling to herself. Tom had taken her hand as they climbed the castle stairs and even though she did not need his help to climb the stairs she accepted it because holding Tom's hand was a good feeling. She really liked him and wondered if he liked her. She hoped he did.

Tom had asked her if she had told her parents about their friendship and said that he had told his parents that he had met someone very nice in the Library who was helping him with his research. His mother then asked him where Eleanor lived in Newcastle and she was satisfied when told she lived in Summerhill. That was a good address and that mattered to Norah, his mother.

Chapter 4

That evening when Eleanor got home her family were all seated around the big dining table in the dining room. It was quite unusual for the whole family to be eating their evening meal together. They were all doing different things now that they had grown up, and did not always go to their parents' house for the evening meal but because it was their father's birthday the whole family had made an effort to be there. They knew their parents loved to see the whole family together and enjoyed listening to their chatter. As young adults there was plenty to talk about, and there was no lack of conversation as they exchanged news and offered opinions on various matters of the day.

Eleanor and Benjamin were the only members of the family living at home now, although sometimes James the doctor son came home to get some sleep, if he had been on call the previous night and was too tired to walk to his own home in Jesmond. Two other brothers, Frank and Harry had also moved out of the family home as they pursued their careers and they now had their own accommodation.

Eleanor looked hard at her mother as they ate the meal that evening and thought she looked a bit strained, Ever since that morning last week, when her mother had behaved so bizarrely, she had been observing her mother closely but so far her mother was behaving as if it had never happened. Was she ever going to reveal her secret? In her view the whole family should know. She did not like being the only one who knew what her mother had done.

Her mother was quiet at the family meal considering she had always enjoyed joining in the conversation and listening to all the comings and goings of her family. Perhaps it was because she was plucking up courage to tell the family now, Eleanor thought, but the meal ended without her saying anything about it. Eleanor felt unhappy about it all. It was a secret she did not want to keep. She was wishing that she had not gone out with Benjamin that fateful morning, a few weeks ago, because then she would not have witnessed the scandalous thing her mother had done. What was it her grandmother Nelly used to say to her? 'The truth will out' and so she would just have to be patient until it did. Nelly also used to say, 'You can run away from people and situations, but you can never run away from yourself'. Well that was certainly true Eleanor thought to herself.

Then her brother Frank asked a question, 'Mother, is Auntie Izzy OK? Father told me that you went to Carlisle to see her recently. How did you manage to get there?'

'By train of course. We are in the railway age now, Frank and what a blessing it is.'

Certainly a network of railways was building up throughout the country. The "Newcastle and Carlisle Company" was formed in 1825, and they built a line from Newcastle upon Tyne in the East, to Carlisle in the West. Trains carrying minerals were operating between Blaydon and Hexham in 1834 and the following year in 1835 trains were allowed to carry passengers. Muriel was on one of those trains when she went to visit her sister.

She explained, 'I went by train because I wanted to see what it was like travelling in a train rather than a horse driven omnibus.so I walked down to the Central Station and took the train to Carlisle. It is a brilliant way to travel because it is so much faster. We should be very proud of the two brilliant engineers, George Stephenson and his son Robert, who are mainly responsible for this new form of transport. They were born in the North East.'

Eleanor broke into the conversation. 'I am a little surprised to see you back so soon Mother because I thought you were going to stay with your sister for a few weeks to help with her new baby.' Eleanor wondered what her mother would say to that.

'Well,' said her mother. 'It turned out that Elizabeth, Izzy's older daughter, who has a house in York, came home to help her, so I was not really needed. I stayed a little over a week but was glad to come home. I am too old to look after babies now. I had hardly any sleep because the baby seemed to be awake most of the night. It was really good luck that Elizabeth's boyfriend was coming up to Newcastle on business and he brought me home would you believe, in his horse and cart. That is why I came home so early in the morning. I had to fit in with his arrangements. It was rather an uncomfortable ride but I survived.'

The family accepted this explanation but Eleanor could not understand why her mother was lying and why she could not be honest. She was sure that as a family they could face the truth and deal with it.

'It was strange without you, my dear even for such a short time,' Cyril commented. 'I am so glad that you are back, even though I never heard you come in that morning. That is not really surprising because you know how soundly I sleep. Never mind, you got home for my birthday and I am so glad.'

Cyril was so happy to have his family with him on his birthday and he looked around them with pride. His four sons were growing into manhood very maturely although there were concerns about the health of his youngest son, Benjamin. James, the eldest son, born in 1862, had recently qualified as a doctor from Durham University Medical School and had just taken up a post at Newcastle General Hospital. He hoped eventually to specialise as a Paediatrician, which would mean working with children. That would be later, of course, when he had gained more experience. He worked hard and Cyril was sure his son would have a very successful career. Frank, the second eldest son born in 1864, was very interested in trains which perhaps was not too surprising, having been born at a time when the great men who pioneered railways were born and trains were becoming the new mode of transport. Frank wanted to study engineering with a view to working as an engineer on the railways. Harry, the third son, born in 1866 was interested in a naval career and was attending a Naval College at South Shields. Benjamin, his youngest son, born in 1868 was unfortunately not so robust as his brothers. He was prone to asthma attacks and suffered frequently from chest infections.

This could have been hereditary because his mother Muriel had suffered all her life from chest infections and asthma. The latter had caused her many frightening moments when she was having a prolonged asthma attack. There had been times when she had felt she was choking and could not breathe, but Cyril was very good at calming her down when this happened and he had actually once saved her life with his very prompt attention. Her mother Nelly once told Cyril that she dreaded the winter every year because Muriel's chest was much worse in the cold weather. Fortunately, as she grew older her chest infections became less frequent and she had fewer asthma attacks. In fact, he could not remember when she had her last attack but it certainly was not recently. He was pleased that Benjamin was looking really well at the moment.

Cyril knew that Benjamin was bullied at school from what his sons had told him. He could not stand up for himself which was a pity because the bullies took advantage of that. Benjamin's stooped shoulders because of his asthma and chest infections and his frequent absences from school also made him a target for scoffing taunts. 'Mummy's Boy' or 'Cissy' were their favourite taunts to shout after him and he hated it, almost as much as he hated his brothers having to stand up for him, although he knew they were just being protective.

He was not as academic as his brothers but his father knew he had other skills and was a very kind, thoughtful and loving young man. He never made any reference to his bad health and certainly was never sorry for himself. He never wanted to be treated any differently from his brothers or sister.

When Cyril looked at his youngest child he always felt emotional. She was the daughter for whom he and his wife

Muriel had longed after four sons. She was born in 1873 and was a very pretty baby. Her brothers loved her. She had made their family complete. They had called her Eleanor because it was a family name on Cyril's side of the family and for generations the first daughter born into any of their families had to be called Eleanor. Muriel had hoped her daughter would inherit her white-blonde very curly hair, but only Benjamin had blonde hair and it was not curly.

Cyril remembered his daughter's birth very clearly. Muriel had gone into labour earlier than expected putting Cyril into a panic because he was well aware of the dangers surrounding childbirth in the 19th century. Some births ended in the loss of the baby and even the mother. Muriel had not been at all well during her pregnancy which was making him very anxious about her and the baby. He was glad that Nelly, Muriel's mother, was staying with them because she was a very capable woman. She had had six children of her own and certainly knew a lot about childbirth with its accompanying fears. She had even delivered babies where she lived on the Side. In fact, a lot of people were very grateful for all the things she could do, such as helping their sick children, applying splints to broken limbs before hospital treatment and even 'laying out' their dead. Nelly was not too worried about the doctor getting there on time because if necessary she could deliver the baby herself.

Cyril had to go out in a blizzard to fetch the doctor. He was muttering to himself that this would have to be their last baby because he could not go through all this worry again. The pregnancy had been very tiring for Muriel with four young sons to look after and he and Muriel had already decided that this would be their last child. Cyril was quite glad about this because he had to admit that he was not good with babies. He enjoyed them more when they were older and not so demanding. He hated the sleepless nights and incessant crying. Muriel on the other hand loved babies and had had plenty of experience in looking after babies being the eldest of six siblings. Motherhood suited her.

Cyril and the Doctor were a long time in coming because of the weather conditions, but they were in time for the Doctor to deliver a perfect baby daughter. 'She is small,' the doctor said, 'but perfectly formed.' Her proud parents repeated those words many times when they were introducing their beloved baby daughter. 'The doctor said she is small but perfectly formed.' They were so proud of her.

Chapter 5

E leanor was very special from her birth. She had grown into a beautiful young person not only in looks but with an inner beauty. She was passionate about books like her father, loved children and enjoyed music, although she had not inherited her mother's beautiful singing voice. That was definitely a gift which Muriel often used when her children were babies, singing lullabies to help them to sleep. Eleanor may not have been able to sing beautifully but she had the gift of sensitivity with regard to people. She could empathise with them and this was particularly true with regard to her youngest brother, Benjamin. She spent a lot of time with him because he was so unsure of himself. She knew that he felt inferior to his academic brothers and sister which was nonsense of course. He needed constant reassurance that he was equal to his brothers. She explained to him that everyone is different, and he had qualities which were special to him.

'Everyone is unique,' she told him. 'There is no one person like anyone else in the whole universe and everyone should embrace their uniqueness.'

'What do you mean by that, Eleanor?' Benjamin had asked.

'Well you do not worry about what other people can do but concentrate on what you yourself can do and do it to the best of your ability. Now you, Benjamin, have gifts that your brothers do not have. You can draw and sketch very skilfully and paint beautiful pictures, so yours are artistic talents. Your brothers cannot do what you can do and you cannot do what they can do but it does not matter because we are all individuals with our skills and talents and must value one another. Our parents would be horrified if they thought you felt yourself inferior to your siblings. They love us all equally. Now do you understand what I am saying, Benjamin?'

'I do and thank you for telling me that and for listening to me as you do. You always help me with my doubts and insecurities. I am going to try to be a more confident person from now on.'

'That's the spirit,' Eleanor replied.

Eleanor's next words brought a smile to his face. 'Have I ever told you, Benjamin, that I think you are the most handsome of my brothers. You are tall, slim and have beautiful blond hair which you keep shoulder length and in perfect condition. You also have very blue eyes with very long lashes which I envy enormously. My friends are always commenting on your good looks. You have no need to be so negative about yourself.'

Benjamin loved being in Eleanor's company. She cheered him up all the time and he much preferred her company to that of his brothers, because the latter enjoyed more active pursuits and he just did not have the energy sometimes to join in. He enjoyed walking, which is why Benjamin and Eleanor were often seen walking together in Leazes Park, the first public park in Newcastle, which opened in 1872. Sometimes they walked on the Town Moor, a huge space of grassland in the middle of Newcastle and if they were feeling energetic they walked to Jesmond Dene, which was their favourite place because it was so picturesque and Benjamin found a wealth of material for his sketches and paintings. It was a long walk from their home to Jesmond Dene and sometimes it was a struggle for Benjamin with his breathing problems, but Eleanor insisted that the exercise was good for him. They both loved Jesmond Dene, especially sitting somewhere near the waterfall beside the ruin of what used to be a mill. They also liked to walk across the stepping stones, taking bets as to who would fall in the water first. Neither of them had done that so far but there was always a first time!

Sometimes her three oldest brothers and herself rode on their bikes to Jesmond Dene. It was much quicker than walking although it excluded Benjamin because cycling required a lot of breath and energy. He always said that he did not mind at all not going with them. Cyril had bought each of his children a bicycle except Benjamin, who was free to borrow one of his brothers' bikes if he felt up to using it. The first pedal bikes appeared in 1839 and cycling very soon became a favourite national pursuit. Cycling clubs were set up in many towns.

When she and James, Frank and Harry rode to Jesmond Dene, when they were teenagers, they had a wonderful time together. They explored all the different paths and loved hiding from one another behind all the trees and undergrowth. Sometimes if they had any energy left, they walked up the steep pathways to 'Paddy Freemans Park' which looks out over the dene. It was a lovely park with a lake and lots of green grass and trees.

Her brothers were such good fun and teased her mercilessly at times but it was always in good humour. It had been wonderful growing up with four brothers. They all got on extremely well and were very protective of her, despite their teasing. April 1st was the day they teased her the most. They always managed to catch her out with one of their pranks and then took great delight in shouting April Fool. It was maddening at the time but she soon got over it.

Eleanor had had a few boyfriends and her brothers always 'checked them out' as they called it. It annoyed her at times because she was perfectly capable of choosing someone herself, but they took their role of protection very seriously.

A case in point was when Harry asked her a question on the evening of her father's birthday. He wanted to know who the young man was that he had seen her with beside the Swing Bridge.

'I was down on the quayside and saw you,' Harry said. 'Remember I spend an awful lot of time beside the river because I love boats so much. What were you doing there?'

'It was one of my meetings with Tom, the young man I met in the library. He is interested in the history of Newcastle and I was answering his questions about our city. We are just good friends.'

'He looked nice, I have to say,' Harry said, 'but just be careful.'

'Brothers!' Eleanor thought but she had to admit that she thought a lot about Tom. He seemed to like her and listened intently to her mini-lectures as he called them. He was good

company and she was looking forward to meeting him in the
library the next day.

Chapter 6

The next morning Eleanor took care choosing what to wear. She wanted to look her best for Tom. It was May and the weather was getting warmer, so she did not need to wear her thick coat. She finally chose her fashionable blue linen dress with a long skirt and neat long-sleeved bodice with a cream high frilled neckline, which she thought suited her best. After some consideration she decided that even though it was warm, she would wear her matching blue bonnet with satin ribbons to tie under her chin, for no other reason than that she liked herself in it. She was taking Benjamin with her to meet Tom because Benjamin loved going to the library and he wanted to meet Eleanor's new friend.

As they were leaving the house her mother commented on their appearances.

'Eleanor, you look very smart and pretty, as you always do and Benjamin you are looking very smart and so handsome.'

They make a very good-looking pair, Muriel thought. Benjamin was not quite as tall as his brothers who were all over 6 feet, but he was still tall and very attractive with his long blonde shoulder length hair and vivid blue eyes. Eleanor always dressed well and was very pretty. Her dark brown hair was wavy and very unlike her own. Not for the first time Muriel wondered from whom she had inherited her mass of blonde curls. The trouble was, people called them corkscrew curls because they were so tight and when she was very young, other children used to shout after her ' How are your corkscrew curls today Muriel?' or 'Have you found your corkscrew yet, Muriel?' and worst of all was when they shouted one word 'Corkscrew' over and over again. Everyone laughed when they did that. She put up with it, but she did not like it and sometimes it was very hard not to cry. She hated her curls and was the only one of her siblings to have them. She was glad that none of her own children had inherited her tight curls, but she would have liked one of them to love singing as much as she did and to have her beautiful singing voice, but so far not one of her children had shown any interest in singing. 'You used to sing like an angel,' her father had once told her. She loved singing, especially if there was an audience. When her grandmother entertained friends she always wanted Muriel to sing to them and she loved doing that. One of the ladies told her that she had perfect pitch, but she was not sure what that meant at the time until her granny told her it was a compliment, meaning her singing was good. It made her feel so happy. Her grandmother always told her that it was good to say nice things about people and if you could not say anything nice then it was better to say nothing at all.

Looking at Eleanor and Benjamin on their way out that day had reminded Muriel of another baby whom she would never see grow up and that brought back all the heartache of a few weeks ago.

She had tried to put the whole incident to the back of her mind but it was not as easy as she thought and the hardest thing to bear was the guilt. She had no-one with whom to share that guilt and the only place where she could give vent to her feelings was in church, which is why she made frequent visits to St Matthew's Church, near where she lived, and sobbed uncontrollably.

When she had her dark days she was so glad that Eleanor was still at home. They had always been close and able to talk about anything that was troubling them, but she could not possibly share her present problem with her daughter. It was too shocking and she could not bear it if her daughter knew what she had done. It could ruin their relationship. It would have to remain a secret. Muriel actually felt a sense of guilt that she had not told her daughter the truth about her visit to her sister's in Carlisle. She had said in the past that they could go together to see her sister and new baby but it had been impossible to take her to Carlisle this time. She knew Eleanor would be hurt and that could be why she was being rather distant with her. It was strange too that Eleanor had not told them anything about her new boyfriend. Normally Eleanor delighted in telling them all that was going on in her life. That was the joy of Eleanor. She was open and honest and full of life and having a new boyfriend would have been great news to share and talk about, but their daughter had not opened up about him at all. She was definitely subdued to the extent that her father noticed. He even commented to Muriel that he hoped all was well with Eleanor because she did not seem her normal exuberant self.

'I will make sure that I have a good chat with her very soon,' Muriel promised. 'She is sure to tell me if anything is the matter.' Having said that, Muriel had to admit that she was being very underhand to keep a secret from her daughter. It made her think of the time her mother Nelly had told her about a secret she had kept from her daughter, although it was trivial compared with Eleanor's secret. It went back to the baptism of Muriel who was Nelly and Robert's first child. Nelly wanted to call the baby Muriel after her own mother, but Robert insisted that she should be called Eleanor after his mother. In the end Muriel was called Eleanor Muriel but was always addressed and known as Muriel. When Cyril and Muriel had their own daughter, Cyril had insisted that she be called Eleanor and Muriel was quite happy to agree with that. She actually liked the name better than her own and was quite happy to share a name with her daughter. What she did not know was that Muriel and Eleanor were sharing the same secret.

Thinking back again to that day when she had crept back into the house very early in the morning, Muriel was so relieved that she had not disturbed Cyril. If he was aware of her getting into bed it did not disturb him very much. He grunted, turned over and went back to sleep. He was not expecting her back so early, of course. She would have to think of an explanation the next morning but knowing him as she did, he would not suspect anything because he had always trusted her implicitly. She had felt a pang of guilt looking at him sleeping so peacefully, but convinced herself that she had done it for him because he had not wanted any more babies. However, the truth was she had done it for herself so that she could continue life as she knew it before getting pregnant again at 50. Cyril need never know.

He was a good man and would be appalled at her actions. He might even want to move away from the area, and she could not bear that.

She loved living in Summerhill. It was considered one of the best areas in Newcastle and the people who lived there were considered to be ladies and gentlemen. It was very different from where she had been born and brought up. The Side was in the poorest part of Newcastle near the river, but she was now living in an area surrounded by middle class people and she was blissfully happy. It had always been her ambition to live in a big house in a good area and her ambition had been fulfilled. She often wondered what her parents would say if they could see her now. They would hardly believe it and they would say she had done very well for herself. Her father would have a chuckle if he knew she was even trying to conceal her Tyneside accent and cultivate a more genteel way of speaking.

Summerhill was a perfect area. It was only small and was just off the West Road at the junction of Elswick Road and the West Road. The houses were mainly occupied by Quakers or Jews and were mainly businesspeople who had made their name in one of the numerous industries that had grown up around the River Tyne. The house Cyril had bought in Summerhill was one of nine very substantial, high class terrace dwellings. It had a large front garden and path leading up to the front door and ornate wrought iron railings along the frontage of the house defining the balconies on the upper front rooms. The whole street had a rather grand appearance.

St Matthew's Church stood at the Elswick road entrance to the area.

A big house called 'Summerhill House' used to stand where St Matthew's Church stood now. It was the home of a bookseller who had arrived in the area from a village called Summerhill in Dublin. This house had been burnt down in 1773 but was rebuilt and had had various owners before being demolished. The site where St Matthew's church was built in 1887 was empty when Muriel and Cyril and their family came to live there in 1880.

Cyril took a great interest in the garden, never having had a garden before and he worked hard to make it a very nice entrance to their house. Benjamin was often to be found in the garden sketching or drawing and he had painted in water colour, a lovely picture of the house and garden, showing its beauty and grandness. It had pride of place on the wall of their dining room.

Harry had made friends with a very nice young man who lived in Ravensworth Terrace, Summerhill. This was very near to their house and was a small terrace of attractive houses that ran parallel with the West Road. The latter was one of the main routes out of Newcastle leading to Corbridge and Hexham and ultimately to the county of Westmorland in the Lake District. Eleanor often visited Ravensworth Terrace with her brother when he went to see Phillip who was very knowledgeable about the Summerhill area and she enjoyed talking to him. Muriel encouraged Eleanor and Harry in their friendship with Phillip and his family, as she wanted to be accepted by this more select, educated class of people in Summerhill. She wanted to be middle class and throw off her working class days.

Her rise in status she knew was all because of Cyril. He had worked so hard for his family and only wanted the best for them. He was very well respected and through his hard work had been able to afford this lovely house in Summerhill, where she and her family were so happy. Cyril was the best thing that had ever happened to her and she should never have deceived him. What had possessed her to act in such a deceitful way. She loved him very much and her thoughts went back to when they lived near one another when they were growing up. They had got on so well and she had missed him terribly when he moved away. She had other boyfriends but none of them measured up to Cyril and when they met up again in their late teens their friendship developed into love and they were married in 1860 when Muriel was only 20 years of age. Her parents thought her too young to marry but she was so in love with Cyril and he with her, that they gave their permission. Their marriage was very happy and they had now been married over 30 years.

She knew that she had jeopardised everything because if Cyril ever found out what she had done he would be very angry and heartbroken. It was only now that she fully realised the error of her ways. What she had done was unforgivable and Cyril did not deserve any of it.

Cyril's parents were not as poor as her own and had been able to move away from The Side to Byker, which was in the East of Newcastle. It was also near the Ouseburn Valley which was the site of numerous potteries. Cyril's father was going to work in one of the potteries belonging to the Maling family which was the main reason for their move. Cyril did well at school and even though school was not compulsory until the end of the 19th century he never missed a day at school because he loved it. His father told him all about the potteries as he grew up because he knew Cyril wanted to work in a pottery like his father.

He explained that clay was the basic of every pottery, and cheap clay and brown clay are easily accessed on Tyneside, but it is not the best for making dainty pottery. There are clays of much better quality elsewhere in the country. However the North-East clay is very suitable for the coarser and more robust pottery known as brown ware which is very suitable for everyday home use. This type of pottery became very popular and this coarser clay was exported in large amounts to other countries, which is why pottery had become a booming industry on Tyneside.

There were numerous potteries in the Ouseburn Valley but for Cyril's father the greatest and most successful pottery was the one in which he worked and that was the Maling Pottery. It was a family business which originated in North Hylton in Sunderland. The family brought their business to the Ouseburn Valley and the owner, Mr Robert Maling, opened a completely new factory in 1817 called the Ouseburn Bridge Pottery on the East Bank of the River Tyne. It was a good move and the pottery flourished. Robert Maling was a good boss because he had the best interests of his staff at heart and treated them very well.

His father's hopes for Cyril were fulfilled when Cyril was 16 and started to work at the factory when he left school in 1849. He was a hard worker and enjoyed the work and found his boss Robert Maling was just as his father had described him, a very nice man indeed. The latter soon noticed this bright hard working young man and it was not too long before Cyril was promoted.

In 1853 Robert Maling retired and his brother Christopher Thompson Maling took over the firm. He was very ambitious and he was impressed with Cyril's enthusiasm and interest in the business. He gained another promotion to encourage him to stay in the business. He confided in Cyril that he had plans for building a new much bigger factory. Cyril enjoyed his work and it was near where he now lived but he wanted to move back to the area where he had lived as a child even though it would be quite a journey back to the pottery each morning. He was a keen cyclist and so was undeterred by that and he moved back to The Side area in 1857. He was earning good money now and was able to buy himself a nice house in Sandhill. It was at this time that he became acquainted with Muriel again and after three years of courtship they married in 1860.

Chapter 7

C yril and Muriel had played together as children, a few doors away from each other on The Side. Their parents became friends as did the children and they loved playing games together outside on the cobbles. Elsie, Cyril's mother, made wonderful scones and Muriel was always there on baking day to sample them. As Muriel and Cyril grew up, they became very good friends even though Cyril was seven years older than Muriel. When Cyril's family moved to Byker when he was thirteen years old, Muriel and Cyril missed one another but soon lost touch living so far apart. Cyril never knew that Muriel's family had had to go and live in a workhouse. Muriel never told him because there was a stigma attached to the workhouse which made her feel ashamed. When they met up again in 1857 Muriel still did not tell Cyril because they both got on so well and she was afraid that if he knew he would end their relationship.

Muriel and Cyril were married in 1860 in St Nicholas's church at the top of 'The Side'. They were not religious people but wanted to marry in a church mainly because their parents had done so and tradition was important in Victorian times. Indeed, marriage and family life seemed to have more meaning as the 19th century progressed. This was largely due to Queen Victoria and her husband Prince Albert whom she had definitely married for love. They had nine children and openly showed how much they cared about their children, by spending time with them and even playing with them. Usually this was part of the governess's duties, but Queen Victoria and her husband were setting a new model for family life. Children had a right to be loved and cherished within a family unit and they considerably raised the status of children in society.

This was a good ethic to have but many families in Newcastle did not have that experience because they were too poor. At the beginning and middle of the 19th century the prevalent belief was that children should work and contribute to the family income and in poorer areas children hardly had a childhood. They had to grow up quickly and take on tasks which were far too difficult for them and in many instances children were exploited.

Cyril and Muriel had passed St Nicholas's church many times when they were growing up on The Side but had never been inside. It was a big church and when Cyril went to see the vicar of the church to ask about being married there, he asked him to tell him a little about the church.

'I am an historian you see, and feel sure this church has an interesting history,' Cyril said.

'Indeed it has, Mr Delaney,' replied the vicar. 'Let us start with the name. Do you know how the church got its name? It is named after the Patron Saint of Sailors and Boats who was called Nicholas. The church dates back to the 11th century. It was built in 1091 shortly after William the Conqueror's son had completed building the castle which was to give this town its name. It would have been a wooden church but was rebuilt in stone in the twelfth century. Unfortunately, it was damaged by fire in 1216 but was restored in 1359. Now anything else you would like to know?'

'Yes,' Cyril said. 'You have not mentioned the tall tower.'

'That tower,' the vicar continued, 'is rather unique. It was added to the church in 1448 and is called a Lantern Tower because it served as a navigation point for ships using the River Tyne for over 500 years. A barrel of tar was placed in the lantern to provide light. The tower is one of only a few that were built in a certain style known as a Scottish Crown. The style originated in St Giles Church in Edinburgh which is where the name "Scottish Crown" originated. Come outside and I will show you.'

They went outside and looked up at the tower.

'Can you see a spire rising out of the tower? If you look carefully you will see that the spire holds a lantern shape object. For centuries ships coming into shore were guided by its light and were able to see clearly if there was anything hazardous in their way nearer the shore. It is said to have guided many ships to safety and so you can see that it is a special tower. Now remember I said it was built in the style of a Scottish Crown. Well look closely again and you can see that the structure of the spire from the base takes on the shape of a crown and this is likened to the crown which was put upon the head of Jesus when he was crucified.

'Now back we go inside. I hope that has been helpful, Mr Delaney. Is there anything else you want to know?'

'Thank you very much, vicar, for all that you have told me but could I just ask if there are any other unique features?'

'Well I remember you saying that you liked books, so you might like to know that in 1736 a library was added to this church. It was called the 'Tomlinson Library' after the man who gave 7000 books to it. He was called Dr Tomlinson and his books were so special that it was feared they might get stolen and so they were chained to the wall. The chains are still there but they are cumbersome and not very attractive. The library was not well used and so the library was closed – which is a pity because no doubt you would have been interested in it.'

'Just one more thing, vicar. Is it true that Lord Collingwood of naval fame was baptised and married in this church because he lived on The Side where I lived as a boy?'

'Yes it is true, Mr Delaney, and there is a bust of him and a plaque telling all about him inside the Cathedral, which you might like to go and see. He was a remarkable man, born in 1748, who went to sea when he was only 13 years of age and spent most of his life at sea.

'He was one of the heroes in the Battle of Trafalgar who took command of the ship after Lord Nelson was killed. There was a terrible storm after the battle but under the command of Lord Collingwood no British ships were lost.

'It was very sad that he died at sea as he was trying to get back to England where he wanted to die.'

Cyril interrupted the vicar to say, 'The Side residents are immensely proud that Lord Collingwood was born and lived on their street. They think it gives added status to the area.'

'Well I think it does really and now I am afraid I have to go as I have a meeting, but thank you for your interest in this church and for wanting to be married in it. I will look forward to conducting your marriage service in our lovely church..'

'Thank you very much, vicar, for all the information you have given me. I am glad that this church has survived to this day because I heard that it went through a period of dereliction and fire damage in the 13th and 14th centuries. I am greatly looking forward to being married in such an historic church.'

Cyril took Muriel to see the church before they got married and she also was impressed with the building and was very excited about being married there.

Chapter 8

After their wedding Cyril and Muriel lived in the house Cyril had bought in Sandhill when he moved back to The Side in 1857. Muriel knew a little bit about Sandhill from her father. He had explained it on one of their walks when she was a young girl. He told her that because the River Tyne was a tidal river, a heap of sand used to be exposed when the tide was out, at the place where the Lort Burn, a tributary of the River Tyne, joined the river. The area around it was then given the very apt name of Sandhill.

'What did they do with all that sand, Father?' Muriel had wanted to know. "Because there is no heap of sand now.'

Her father explained that the heap of sand had been dealt with in the 1300s when land reclamation and culverting work took place and a road was created there. Houses were later erected and by the 17th century the bigger houses were owned by wealthy merchants and businessmen, who had their warehouses and offices on the quayside. It became a very fashionable place to live and was a centre for the town's businesses and commercial trading and for the social life of the town.

Markets were held there selling fish, herbs, bread, cloth and leather. It was a place of recreation and festivals were celebrated there.. There was even a bull ring until 1768 when a spectator was gored by a bull and died from his injuries. The ring was then closed.

'What a terrible thing to happen, Father,' Muriel said. 'What is that big, rather stylish building which faces onto the Sandhill area with its back to the quayside?'

Her father informed her that it was an important building and was called the Guildhall. 'It is the Civic Headquarters of the town where administrative work is done. It is the centre for Newcastle Guilds and contains Law Courts. The very first building on the site was in 1235 and it was in that year that King Henry the Third granted Newcastle a Merchant Guild because it was an expanding market town. The Merchant Guild controlled the way in which trade was conducted in the town and as a result quickly became the most powerful, economic political force in Newcastle.

'This original building from 1235 was still in existence in 1425 when Roger Thornton, a Newcastle businessman, built the hospital of St. Catherine on the east end of that building. Then in 1658, Robert Trollope, another businessman, built a much grander Guildhall with a new courtroom and meeting place for the Lord Mayor, Sheriff and Aldermen to have their meetings. Finally in 1825 John Dobson, the famous architect in Newcastle, extended the eastern end of the building and the completed building is the one we see now. It has quite a history.'

'I will show it more respect, Father, now that I know its importance. But I need to ask you another question. Do you know anything about fishwives and the Guildhall building?'

'Yes I can help you with that question. Did I ever tell you that my uncle's father was once Lord Mayor of Newcastle? Well it is he who handed down this story. I have heard it many times. It concerns the famous architect John Dobson. He was asked to make some changes to the Guildhall building in 1825, as I have just said, and one of the things he did was build a little colonnade on the west side of the building, which almost looked out over the river. He did this for the fishwives who sold fish beside the river day after day in all weathers. He built the colonnade so that they could shelter there in very bad weather. Apparently, they were very disdainful about it at first, but then a spell of rainy weather convinced them that it was a good thing and they made good use of it after that. A new fish market was later built very near the High Level Bridge and the colonnade on the Guildhall was filled in and so you cannot see the colonnade to day.'

Muriel was still curious and wondered if her father knew what the inside of the building looked like.

'I am told very impressive,' her father said. 'Someone with whom I used to work at the shipyard had to attend the magistrate's court in the Guildhall recently and he said it is beautiful inside. It has a beautiful tiled floor depicting the history of Newcastle and there is a fantastic sweeping staircase. He said it was quite an experience being in the magistrate's court but rather intimidating with a pair of shackles for immediate use if necessary, hanging there for all to see.'

They had had a most interesting walk that day and before walking up to The Side where they then lived, Muriel wanted to know about the five beautiful timber framed houses which they were passing.

'Those houses were built for wealthy men and they are all four or five storeys high and as you can see are all timber framed. They nearly all contain timber which dates from the 1500s but I am told they were restored in the 1620s You can see their entire frontage is occupied by windows. They are lovely houses. I would like to have been able to afford to buy a house in Sandhill for my family, but I never earned enough money to do that.'

'Father, stop worrying about that. We were all happy living on The Side and you have always done the very best you could for us.'

Walks with her father were always good when she was young. Her father always made them interesting and it was true that her father worked very hard to feed and clothe his family. When Muriel married Cyril she knew he would be just like her father Robert who was also a hardworking man. Cyril had to make the journey back to Ouseburn Valley for work every day but he never complained.

Muriel could hardly believe she was living on Sandhill. It was so different from The Side. They had not lived there very long when someone told them the story of Bessie Surtees, who had lived in one of the big timber-framed houses. Bessie was described as a 'beautiful young woman'. Her father was a wealthy banker who had been Lord Mayor of Newcastle several times and his daughter Bessie, when 17 years of age, had fallen in love with a young man called John Scott who was 22 years old and a coal fitter. He wanted to marry her, but Bessie's father did not approve of the young man and wanted her to end the relationship. This she refused to do and on the 18th of November in 1772, during the night, she climbed out of a window and down a ladder to her waiting boyfriend They hurried to Blackshiels near to Dalkeith in Scotland where they were married.

Shortly after this they returned to Newcastle and were welcomed back although rather reluctantly by Bessie's family. They had an English wedding in St Nicholas's church on January 19th 1773. Although many people had been doubtful about Bessie and John marrying so young, their marriage was very successful. John Scott went on to become Chancellor of Great Britain in 1801 and his son was a pupil at the Royal Grammar School when it occupied a site on Westgate Road.

Muriel loved that romantic story and loved the house they lived in on this very well-respected area of Sandhill. It was a pity she thought, that her father did not live to see her living in this house, but Nelly was a frequent and welcome visitor.

Chapter 9

E leanor and Benjamin met up with Tom in the library
the day after the birthday party and Tom immediately
commented on Eleanor's attractive appearance.

He said, 'Eleanor I do like that blue dress. It matches your
eyes perfectly and your matching bonnet is lovely with those
satin ribbons tying below your chin.'

Tom and Benjamin liked one another immediately. Tom
was very interested in the fact that Benjamin liked painting
because he also enjoyed it and they had a lot to talk about. Tom
even said that he would like Benjamin to paint him a picture of
the River Tyne and the busy Quayside.

Tom also had some interesting news. 'I have made up my
mind about what I am going to do with my future, Eleanor. I
am going to be a teacher and I have applied to go Bede College
in Durham, which is a Church of England Training College
for young men, which opened in 1841. I have decided, you see,
that I did not want just to teach one subject. I want to teach
young people more about the world in which they live and
make history come alive for them. I feel really good about my

choice. I will be able to tell the pupils about all the famous engineers, inventors and entrepreneurs who have been born and lived in Newcastle upon Tyne.

'My parents, of course, wanted me to go to university. My father is a graduate of Oxford University and had high hopes of me sitting the entrance examination and probably getting a place there because even though I say it myself I have done well at school. There have been heated arguments in our household recently when we have discussed the future. I think I told you that I have attended the Royal Grammar School since we moved up here and could easily have taken the entrance examination for Oxford or Cambridge from there but I just did not want to do it. I am quite happy to go to Training College to become a teacher. I feel sure that it is the right thing for me to do at this stage in my life.'

'I hope your parents are not too cross, Tom, or think that I have influenced you in any way.'

'Of course not, Eleanor. They know nothing about you anyway. I have only told them that I have a library friend whom I enjoy seeing. I am being true to myself and that is important to me, so do not worry. Now do you think I will make a good teacher?'

'You will make a wonderful teacher, Tom. I just know that you will be a success in whatever you do and it means that you will not be too far away and we will still be able to see one another in the holidays. I am pleased about that.'

'Well so am I,' Tom said. 'I have enjoyed your company over the last weeks, so why don't we meet up again tomorrow and talk more about it? I want to get to know you better and we could have a walk along the river and look at the bridges or visit the Cathedral again. Your parents were married there, weren't they?'

'Yes but it was not a cathedral when they were married. It was given that status in 1882, when the Diocese of Newcastle was formed and Newcastle was designated a city, the following year.'

Eleanor smiled all the way home and her parents commented on her good humour. Benjamin also seemed very happy.

'You have both had a good day obviously,' Muriel said. 'You will have to tell us all about it over dinner.'

But Eleanor found herself not wanting to share things with her mother now. She still wanted an explanation of her mother's actions, though her hopes of this were fading rapidly as time went on. Her mother's secret remained her secret and the ache in her heart also remained.

Fortunately Benjamin took his mother's attention when he told her that they had been talking to a very nice boy who was a friend of Eleanor's and he wanted Benjamin to paint him a picture of the River Tyne showing all the ships and different kinds of boats that sail up and down it.

'That is great, son,' his mother said. 'You can now tell everybody that you have been commissioned to paint a picture. That does not happen to every artist so you have done very well indeed. Your father will be as delighted as myself. Well done, Benjamin. If I like your painting of the River Tyne you will have to paint another one for our house. You know how much I like the River Tyne. Now, Eleanor, it is your turn to tell me about your day.'

'Not tonight, Mother. I am tired,' Eleanor replied. 'Another time perhaps.'

Again Muriel had that feeling that something was not quite right between them. Normally Eleanor would have told her all about what was happening in her life but she was very reluctant tonight to talk about anything.

The next day Eleanor was looking forward to meeting Tom as she walked down the West Road past the Central station, past the Literary and Philosophical Library until she came to St Nicholas' Cathedral where she turned right to go as far as the Black Gate and down the castle stairs to the quayside.

Her thoughts turned to the first time they met. It was the day four weeks ago when she was so upset about her mother and he had been so understanding. It had made a sort of bond between them and he had not questioned her or wanted to intrude on her feelings.

Tom's heart skipped a beat when he saw Eleanor waiting for him. She was so nice and pretty and he was definitely attracted to her. He wanted to get to know her better. He felt sure his parents would like her although his mother could be awkward. He had had several girlfriends but his parents and particularly his mother Norah, were very critical of them, although they had approved of their son's friendship with the headmaster's daughter at his last school in London. It was very upsetting when they criticised his friendships with girls. In their eyes, particularly his mother's, no-one was good enough for their son. He was aware that his parents wanted him to marry well and it was essential to them that his wife would have an impeccable background. That was not what Tom wanted. He wanted to marry a sincere, kind girl, preferably pretty, but her past would not matter to him if he loved her and she felt the same about him. He would just have to wait and see, although he already knew that Eleanor was going to be special to him.

Chapter 10

Tom and Eleanor sat against a bollard beside the Swing Bridge that afternoon and talked about themselves for a little while. Eleanor wanted to talk over with Tom what she had decided for her own future.

'Tom, when you told me you were going to Training College in Durham it made me think a little bit more about what I am going to do with my life and I am pretty sure that I want to train to be a teacher just like you. My parents are always telling me how good I am with my brother Benjamin, who is so unsure of himself, and some of my friends say I am a very patient person and most importantly I love working with children.

'With this in mind I have made some enquiries. I will have to wait two years before I can apply for training college because I am two years younger than you Tom but that does not really matter. We will both have other friends and appreciate each other all the more when we do meet up. One thing worries me and you may already have thought of it. We cannot get home every night from Durham. I think there is a train now which passes through Durham on its way to Newcastle but it does not run too often so we cannot rely on that. It will be your problem soon so what are you going to do? You will have to find somewhere to stay through the week.'

'I will have to talk that over with my parents, Eleanor and I will do that tonight. Thank you for bringing that up.'

'I will have to think about that as well. Tell me what your parents think when I see you tomorrow and by the way I have found out more about the two colleges where we will do our training. There was a Durham Diocese Training School founded in 1839 by Archdeacon Charles Thorp, who had already played a major role in the founding of Durham University in 1832. He proposed a Scheme for Education, which included the creation of a Training School and this school opened in October 1841 in Framwellgate, just outside Durham but it moved to its present site when some land was gifted to the Training School by the Dean and Chapter of Durham. This Training School became a Training College for men in 1865 and during the following year 1866, on the recommendation of Bishop Lightfoot, it was renamed Bede College.

'Then it was proposed that a Training College for females should be built and the site secured for this in 1856 was next to St. Bede's College and would you believe it Tom, Durham Diocese was worried about the two colleges being so close together. I cannot think why – can you?' she said with a smile and a wink. 'The building work began in 1857 and it opened as a Teacher Training College in 1870 but it is only being given the name St Hilds College in 1876, by which time I will be training there. I wonder why it took so long to decide a name for it. I am going to find out when I am a student there.

'Both the colleges are owned by the Church of England and they each have a consecrated Church of England in their grounds. I have also been told that there are stunning views from both colleges over the River Wear looking towards Durham. I am getting excited just talking about it.'

Tom said jokingly 'I will have to be careful then that I do not spend too much time looking at the views or I will get no work done. I am really looking forward to going there and if it all works out we will see one another every weekend. Great!'

'I forgot to say, Tom, that a model school has been built and attached to Bede College which is open to local children and this will give students first-hand experience of teaching, which is really good.'

'It all sounds good, Eleanor and I suggest you and I go to Durham and have a look at both colleges. We will be able to get a train at Newcastle Central Station which will take us through to Durham.'

'That is a great idea,' Eleanor said. 'It will be quite a novel experience for us travelling by train. It is a much faster way to travel, isn't it? I must say that I immensely admire the engineers who are responsible for the railways. I am also immensely relieved that I do not have to go to college any further away than Durham because I thought I was going to have to go to London where the very first Training College was established in 1840. I was a little apprehensive about leaving my family but now I can be very near home. I will miss you when you go away, Tom.'

'I will miss you too, but you will be able to come through to Durham sometimes to see me and I am planning to come home most weekends so that is really good.'

'I agree,' Eleanor said, 'but I suppose in time the colleges will have sleeping accommodation because people will be coming there from other parts of the country. Until then you obviously have to make your own arrangements. Let me know what your parents say after you discuss it with them tonight.'

'What about you and I visiting Durham, Eleanor? It will be a nice day out. Let's do it and let's do it soon.'

They arranged to go the following Saturday. They would be together all day which would give them a chance to talk everything over as well as some sight seeing.

The following Saturday when they were on the train, the first thing Eleanor asked was what his parents had said about accommodation.

'It is good news,' Tom said. 'A colleague of my father's who lives in Durham, by a stroke of colossal luck is looking for a lodger. He has a student living with him at the moment, but that student will be leaving at the end of the summer term. My parents went to Durham to view the property and were impressed with the accommodation and so it is all settled. I will be able to move in when the present student moves out. Isn't that just the best news, Eleanor?'

'Absolutely great, Tom. Problem solved. I am so pleased for you.'

They had a lovely day together visiting the colleges and then sitting by the river and walking along the riverside footpath. They talked about all sorts of things including their future in education.

Eleanor said how pleased she was to be getting involved in education which in the 19th century was not considered to be of great importance.

'Education is a subject about which I am very passionate, Tom. It is so important. People need to gain knowledge and live meaningful lives. Education can give purpose to life and provide a focus for each day. It can reach all areas of our lives and enables us to grow and develop intellectually, socially, physically, emotionally, and spiritually. I believe education involves the well being of the whole person and is important at all levels of society, but today approaching the end of the 19th century there is a vast difference in Newcastle between the rich and the poor.

'Newcastle has become prosperous through our trading links with all the countries in the world and there are many wealthy men living in this town. They have made their money through the toil of poorer people who have worked for them in coal mines, shipyards, and factories but while many of them live in mansion-style houses, poverty exists on a large scale in working class families. There are so many people uneducated in this town and surely everyone has a right to be educated. Do you agree, Tom?'

'Yes I do, but I have little idea about education in Newcastle upon Tyne, Eleanor. In London where I was born and brought up I was educated in private schools and know very little about education other than in the private sector.

'What is there in place to educate children in Newcastle? There must be schools.'

'Yes schools do exist, but it is getting the children to them that is the problem,' Eleanor replied. 'You see in the poorer areas children do not have much of a childhood. They are viewed more as young adults in that they have to work from an early age to help with the family income. In rural areas children are put to work in the fields almost as soon as they can walk and here in towns women take their babies with them to work because they must work to make money to survive. This of course leaves their older children free to wander the streets while their parents are at work and many of them are very neglected and hungry, which in turn can lead to stealing, bad behaviour, and getting into trouble with the police. It is hard to believe, Tom, but some children are put out on the street early in the morning and told not to come home until they have something to bring home which will benefit their family. It does not have to be food. It could be an item of value stolen from a house or market stall which could then be sold on for a good sum of money. Children were told that they could beg, borrow or steal to get what they wanted. There were no standards of behaviour or moral values.

'My very worst hate is the terrible exploitation of women and children which has existed in this century. Women and children were sent down into the coal mines and forced to do tasks which were too difficult for them. Children were bent double pushing heavy wooden tubs of coal along the coal seams to the pit head. Women too are given back breaking work and many women and children get badly injured and suffer chest infections from breathing in the coal dust. This leads to many premature deaths and reminds me of another dreadful exploitation of children and that is chimney sweeping. I cannot believe that some of the wealthy citizens of Newcastle literally push boys as young as seven up their chimneys with a brush, in order to sweep their chimneys. Many of these boys, known as 'climbing boys' are suffocated or burnt to death. How could those people be so cruel?'

Eleanor's voice started to waver as she said this and she had to stop talking. Tom could see that she was getting upset and drew her gently towards him saying 'Eleanor, you are so sensitive and that is why you care so much, but don't worry because neither of those exploitations can happen now. If you remember in 1842 a Miners Act was passed and it banned women and children from working in coal mines and boys working as chimney sweeps.'

'That's right, Tom, I had forgotten about that and I feel happier now, but you do see that some children at the beginning and middle of this century particularly had a very raw deal. They needed to be taken from the streets and put somewhere where they would be protected, looked after and be taught to read and write.'

'That brings us nicely to places of education again, Eleanor. What was the schooling system in Newcastle at the beginning of this century?'

'Well there were schools in the 18th century, some of which were still operating at the beginning of this century, but the problem was they charged a fee which many poor people cannot afford. There were no state or government schools and so there had to be a charge because schools need money to exist; but what I find worrying, Tom, is that there are no qualified teachers in any of the schools and certainly no inspections of the quality of teaching.'

'We are going to put that right, Eleanor by going to college. We are doing something very worthwhile with our lives and that is a good feeling. Now I am still curious about schools in Newcastle at the beginning of this century.'

'I will start with the Dame Schools, Tom. They existed in the 18th century and were still the main providers of basic elementary education for children at the beginning of this century, especially those from very poor homes who could not read or write. They taught the three basic skills, reading, writing and arithmetic. These schools were set up usually in villages and usually by women in their later years and with no formal training in education. They had to have a house big enough for at least ten children up to the age of 14 and they charged a small fee. These schools were popular despite the fee because the classes were small and were held in a nice house. They were flexible too, allowing the parents to take their children out of school when they wanted them to work. When the state schools for elementary education were established in the 1870s Dame Schools ceased to exist.

'My mother Muriel always said that if she had had money and a big house she would have liked to set up a Dame School. She must have been intelligent because she had taught herself how to read and write and she did try to teach her siblings, but they just would not sit down long enough for her to do any teaching. She said they fidgeted all the time and kept talking and giggling. They obviously could only think of her as their sister, not a teacher and she had to abandon the idea. She still carried on making up stories to tell the children at bedtime. One of her brothers called Archie, who was five years old at the time, absolutely loved her stories and was desperate to learn to read but it was difficult to get hold of suitable books to help him. The library had not been built then, which was such a pity. She said she used to make little word cards to help him and he used to try really hard.

'Another type of school in Newcastle,' Eleanor continued, 'was church based. The church has always played an important part in the provision of education. The priests were the learned members of the communities and deemed very suitable to set up schools in which they could have some authority. In Newcastle, these schools were set up by the four main parish churches in the middle of the century. These were St John's at the foot of the West Road or bottom of Grainger street; St Nicholas's near the old Black gate and Castle Keep; St. Andrew's in Gallowgate, reputed to be the oldest church in Newcastle; and All Saints Church, a distinctive building very near the River Tyne.

'These schools were later called Charity Schools and were first and foremost for the convenience of parents and babies as young as two years old were accepted. The very young ones were cared for, fed and taught rhymes and the older children were taught the 3 'R's These charity or church schools were free and they obviously had merit because in 1833 the government gave grants to church schools for their further development.

'It was to this type of school at St John's church, that my mother eventually took her siblings. It was quite a long walk for them, up The Side to Mosley Street, turn left towards the Cathedral and walk up from there towards the Central Station. They then had to bear right within sight of the Central Station towards the West Road and St. John's Church is on the righthand side. She persevered in taking them because she was able to be involved in basic teaching herself and generally looking after the children which she loved.

'Now, Tom, this is interesting. The schools that were by far the best attended were the Sunday Schools, which were set up by the philanthropist Robert Raikes in 1780. Remember I said that children were expected to contribute to the family income by working but Sunday was the Sabbath Day and they did not have to work on that day so they could go to school, Sunday School.

'It has to be said that philanthropists and wealthy industrialists contributed generously to these schools and this could have influenced their popularity but nevertheless, children were given a basic grounding in reading, writing and religion. They were made familiar with the printed word of the Bible and were given all kinds of religious material to distribute. The sad thing is that there were some children who were too poor, ragged and dirty and extremely neglected to be admitted into these Sunday Schools.

'This leads me nicely on, Tom, to the main types of school at the beginning and middle of this century, and to my mind these were the schools which were the best in recognising children's specific needs. They were called the Ragged and Industrial Schools. These schools, together with Reformatories, and Refuges, were all established from the 1840s and in 1844 the Ragged School Union was formed. The Ragged Schools taught reading, writing and arithmetic and girls learned to sew and cook while boys did woodwork and shoemaking. There were other matters to address in Ragged Schools because they opened their doors to all children, regardless of their appearance and behaviour. There are reports of some very bad behaviour in these schools, but no-one was refused entry. Many of them were filthy, dressed very scantily, wretched, frightened and starving. They had to be washed very thoroughly and often their hair was shaved off to get rid of lice They were given clothes, which were stamped with the name of the school to stop their parents taking them to the pawn shop, and best of all they were given a simple meal consisting of soup and occasionally meat, bread and cheese, milk and tea. Apart from lessons, outings were arranged such as day trips to the seaside or country, all free of charge. These schools provided free basic instruction, meals and clothing for thousands of poor children until board schools replaced them in 1870.

'The Ragged Schools believed in manual work and education as the way to save abandoned children and of course they were free. A Council of Education was set up in 1844 and retained the right to examine and certify Ragged Schools throughout their history.

'The Industrial schools were founded to give education, food, lodging and training in the habits of work to convicted children who had not yet served a prison sentence. Remember I said previously that the children who roamed the streets got into trouble with the police and some were taken into custody. The Industrial Schools were trying to educate children before they got into trouble and they trained, educated, fed and cared for children over the age of six but under 12 on entry, though I did hear that in 1884 the upper age limit was raised to fourteen, by one of the later Industrial Schools Acts. The Industrial Schools were non-denominational but the Bible had to be taught

'A Ragged and Industrial School' designed by John Dobson opened in Newcastle on New Road later called City Road in 1854 and was paid for by a group of philanthropists. Eventually about 250 boys and girls attended the school in roughly equal numbers. The boys were taught printing, tailoring, sack and mat making and other practical skills while the girls learnt to make clothes and learn about the duties of Domestic servants. It would seem there were no discipline problems and corporal punishment was hardly ever given. The three 'R's were taught and the children were fed regularly and like the Ragged Schools the Industrial Schools were free. The Ragged Schools eventually received government grants.

'Tom, I am going on far too long about schools but I just need to mention another school which was important to Newcastle and that is the Royal Jubilee School on New Road (later called City Road) which was the first building designed by John Dobson and was opened in 1810 to commemorate the 50th year of the reign of King George the third. It was a boys school and was maintained by private subscriptions with help from the corporation. It was devoted entirely to the education of the poor. Its purpose was to teach reading, writing and arithmetic and to get to know the Bible. The school was given much support and this led to the building of a similar school for girls two years later. The school was run on the same lines as the boys school except that the girls were taught needlework as well as the three 'R's. In 1827 there were 204 pupils on the books. School of course was still not compulsory at this time but paying a fee for education usually meant good pupil attendance.

'It was not until 1870 that an Education Act set up a nationwide network of Board schools but it still did not make elementary education compulsory. It did, however, state that local authorities had the power to make their schools compulsory if they so wished and Newcastle Authority did decide to make school attendance compulsory.

'Another Education Act in 1880 made school compulsory for children aged 5-10 years although the leaving age was raised to 13 at a later date.

'Unfortunately, compulsory education led to a truancy problem and this got so bad that Truancy Officers had to appointed, and I think that was good, Tom, because at last Education was being taken seriously. Everyone, whether poor or rich, was being given the chance of an education.'

Chapter 11

❛All very interesting, Eleanor. I think I am getting to know you better. Four things are very clear. You love books, you love history, you love your family and you feel passionately about certain issues such as education. You are also a very sensitive soul and I like that, because it means you are a caring person.'

'What do you think you have learnt about me?' Tom wanted to know.

'I think you are very kind because you helped me that morning when I felt so wretched.'

Tom interrupted to say, 'You never told me, Eleanor, why you were so upset. Is it something you can talk about yet?'

'No, I just cannot,' Eleanor replied. One day I might be able to tell you but not yet. I wish I could but it is even beyond my understanding and would be impossible I think for anyone else to understand. Sorry, Tom.'

'Don't worry, Eleanor. When you feel ready to share it I will be there to listen.'

'Tom something else I have learnt about you is that you are very intelligent and a very good listener. It meant so much to me in the library that day that you talked and listened to my brother Benjamin. He has no confidence in himself. But you encouraged him to talk and I am so grateful. You are such a good friend and I like you very much.'

'The feeling is mutual, Eleanor. I have really enjoyed being with you these last few weeks and getting to know you. I want to know more about you, so first question is 'Have you always lived in Newcastle?.'

'Yes, I was born on Sandhill near the quayside and my parents were born on The Side, which is even nearer the river. My mother is one of six children and her parents were not very well off, but they were good people. My mother says there was an abundance of love in their home. Her mother, my grandma Nelly, was always busy, with six children to look after and she told me once that she felt she was always washing , mending, wiping noses and bottoms, bathing cut knees and scraped arms, brushing away tears from little faces, settling quarrels, and listening to tales of woe; but she cared for and loved all her children and said the best thing in the world to her were their hugs and kisses.'

'When did your grandparents marry, Eleanor?'

'In 1820,' Eleanor replied, 'when my grandmother was 21 and my grandfather 25. They were very young but were determined to be together and they wanted to start a family straight away.

'They were delighted when a year after they were married their first child was born and that was my mother Muriel. Apparently, she was completely bald when she was born but her hair grew quickly and was a distinctive white blonde colour. As it grew it became very curly and was distinctively white-blonde. Everyone used to comment on the colour of her hair and her tight curls. She still has that hair though it is not quite so white-blonde now after all these years. My grandmother said they never knew from whom she had inherited the colour and curls. As far as she knew there was no-one else in the family with it, but obviously she had inherited it from someone. The curls were so tight and her siblings always knew when their sister was having it brushed because her screams were piercing.

'She was given the name Muriel in memory of Nelly's mother who had died shortly before her first grandchild Muriel was born. Clearly the new baby had helped my grandmother to deal with her grief, but it was four years before she had felt able to have another baby, making Muriel very much the eldest child. She grew up shouldering a lot of responsibility for her five siblings but as you probably know that is expected of the older child in these Victorian days. My mother did not mind a bit because she loved children, but my grandmother told me that it was not easy bringing up a family on The Side.

'It was the main street at that time which led up from the River Tyne to access the upper regions of Newcastle upon Tyne. When it was first built the street was very steep indeed and had got its name because it was as steep as the side of a hill. Nelly and Robert lived there because they could not afford a bigger house with six children to bring up.

'The houses on The Side were small and cramped for a family of eight and altogether The Side was a rather depressing street and certainly not the healthiest. It was very near the River and there were constant fumes from all the industries which had grown up around the river and from the ships and other vessels that constantly sailed up and down it.

'The upper storey of the houses jutted out into the Street, making them dingy and dark but strangely enough this was of benefit to the cheesemongers and dealers in bacon and butter who had their shops on The Side because their goods were kept cool and protected from the rays of the sun. The Side being very steep meant access to the shops and houses was not easily accessible.

'The idea for a bypass was discussed by the council in the 1780s and the then Town Planner and Architect designed a street to by-pass that very steep hill. Newcastle Corporation built the street and it provided a much more gentle climb and wider road access to the centre of town. The very short steep part of The Side still existed up to the castle stairs, which led up to the old Keep and Gatehouse. The new improved and widened road then carried on up to Mosley Street, near St Nicholas's Cathedral and from there it was an easy walk up Grey Street to Grey's monument in the centre of town. The new road was named Dean Street and there must have been great sighs of relief from those who regularly used the old medieval street. It was so much better for everyone.'

'What about those massive stone piers and railway bridge over Dean Street because they are quite impressive?' Tom wanted to know.

'Well that is a railway viaduct which was built in 1849 around the time the Railway Age was coming into being. Apparently, it is going to be widened in 1893. It is the railway line I mentioned when I was talking about the Keep and Black Gate, because it cuts right through the middle of them. I personally think it gives a sense of grandeur to Dean Street.

'Nelly and Robert were lovely grandparents to my brothers and I. They were very kind people who although poor would help anyone They had worked hard to give their children a good upbringing.

'My own father was born on The Side and his family were poor but not so poor as my mother's family. His family moved to Byker when his father went to work in Malings Pottery in the Ouseburn Valley and when Cyril left school he started work in the same pottery. He did very well there. His work and business acumen was outstanding and he eventually became part of the management of the Maling's Potteries. He was promoted many times from a young age and so was able to buy a very nice house in Sandhill when he returned to The Side in 1857. He was still with the firm in 1879 when another member of the Maling family took over the firm and built a very big Pottery on a fourteen acre site at St. Lawrence not far from the Ouseburn Valley. It had workshops, kilns, mills, warehouses and storage buildings and produced large quantities of tableware, toilet and household items, flower pots and commemorative mugs. Maling also made valuable business links with marmalade producer Keiller of Dundee to supply their jars and with Ringtons of Heaton in Newcastle who wanted tea caddies, teapots and other articles. My father told me that Malings produced an impressive nine million items each year. He was very proud of his involvement with this firm.

You and I are very fortunate Tom to be born into families who could educate us well. My brothers and I went to good schools.I really loved Dame Allan's School which I attended in the west end of Newcastle.

'My grandfather Robert had not even had the opportunity to go to school but he had picked things up as he went along and could read and write. He had also got himself a good job at the Elswick shipyard owned by Lord Armstrong and this enabled him to provide well for his six children. He was so proud of that and all six of his children were well dressed and well fed. He was a true Victorian father who took his role as provider of his family very seriously.

'Nelly, his wife, was so thankful for that. Robert always handed over his pay packet to her when he came home on pay day. So many women on The Side never saw the money their husbands earned because they had drunk most of it away at the nearest public house on their way home. My grandmother said there were some awful stories of drunken husbands hitting and abusing their wives and children. Sometimes their screams and hysterical outbursts could be heard right up to the top of The Side. My father would have nothing to do with drunken revelry. He loved his family and every morning when he set off for work down The Side he was usually whistling or humming because he considered himself a lucky man. He had a good wife, six good children and a good job. He was not a religious man, but he told me that he very often found himself thanking an Unseen Power for his good fortune, though he would never admit to believing in a Higher Power to anyone. His life was good.

'It therefore came as a dreadful shock when he had an accident at work. Shipyards are dangerous places and there were no health and safety rules in place, so he was facing a tough time ahead when he was not able to go back to work. He had tripped over a pile of tools which some careless person had left lying on the floor and one of the tools had a sharp blade which embedded in his lower leg. He was rushed to hospital where he had surgery to remove the blade and was found to have also broken his arm and wrist. There were no unemployment or insurance benefits at that time which made Robert extremely worried about money from the onset of his accident. He was not going to be able to provide for his family and that was his worst fear. He was told that he had to rest and that to him was a nightmare. He liked to be busy doing things but his injuries prevented that. As he recovered from the shock of the accident he realised how useless he was now and it was very depressing.

'He was conscious of being in the way when Nelly was busy and he could not help her in any way. She was patient with him at first but the strain began to show when she got irritated and cross with him and the children. She was finding it difficult to feed six children with no-one to bring in a wage. Robert tried to keep out of her way as much as possible and on fine days he sat on a stool outside the front door hoping that someone would come past with whom he could have a good gossip. He was never lonely outside because The Side was a busy street and there was always something to hear or see. He could hear a wooden cart rattling over the cobbles, long before it came into sight and there was no escaping the sound of horses snorting and breathing hard as they pulled heavy carts up the hill. When the horses reached where Robert sat, they often tossed their heads as if wanting to be noticed for the good job they had done climbing up The Side. Women on their way to the small shops which lined the street on either side usually waved and called a greeting to him as they passed. Hooting and hissing noises from the ships were constant as they sailed up and down the busy river. Children's shrill voices could be heard as they called out or shouted to one another while playing their games, usually scantily clad and almost always without shoes. He often heard quarrelsome voices mainly from women whose tempers got frayed with the cramped conditions and unhygienic surroundings. and there was no mistaking the tap, tap of a walking stick. It was a good sign because inevitably such a person stopped for a chat as they recovered their breath after the climb.

'Robert enjoyed his time outdoors even if he had to sit on a stool. All the activity that was going on around him made him feel alive and part of the world again. He tried not to think of how it would have been if he had not had the accident, because that was too much to bear. The word which came to his mind too often was Workhouse. Nelly was finding it harder and harder to feed the children and though she had got herself a little job in one of the shops on The Side, it was still not enough and their money was dwindling fast. Robert was terrified of having to take his family to live in a Workhouse.

'Now, Tom, you know an awful lot more about me. I am out of breath after all that talking.'

Chapter 12

T om and Eleanor had got quite engrossed in their talk about Eleanor's family and Tom suddenly got up and said he would have to dash away because he was having an interview at the library with a view to helping there in some capacity until he went to college.

'That sounds great, Tom. Just think if it were not for the library we might never have met and I would not have liked that.'

'Neither would I, Eleanor. Anyway, I will tell you all about the interview tomorrow. Meet me at our usual place. Swing Bridge at 11.00am. Bye, must dash.'

'I'll be there,' Eleanor shouted after him.

When Eleanor got home her mother was sitting in the garden.

'Come and sit beside me, Eleanor,' she said. 'It seems ages since we had a nice long chat.'

'Mother,' said Eleanor, 'I want to ask you something. Why did you say that day a few weeks ago, on Father's birthday, that you had had to rush off to your sister's in Carlisle? We knew she had had a baby but why did you suddenly have to go and see her? Had she suddenly taken ill and if so how did you know because as far as I know you did not get a letter from her. It gave me a shock when I got home that night and realised you had gone. It was all so sudden.'

Muriel was flustered. She had not expected that question and she had to think quickly.

'I was going for the day only originally and was actually going to ask you to come with me but then purely on a whim I felt I ought to go and see her and the new baby, so I made a very quick decision to go that day. I had no intention of staying as long as I did but when I got there Izzy started to cry and said she was not coping with her new baby, who seemed to cry all time and she was feeling more and more depressed. I had to promise her that I would stay for a few days and that is what I did. Izzy's husband has a job that entails travelling and she is often left on her own. I felt so sorry for her. Fortunately, her older daughter who has her own home now, came to see her while I was there and said she would stay with her mother for a few days. You see Izzy did not intend to have any more children because her other three children are all grown up and she was finding it difficult to bond with her new baby.

'I had told your father that I might be gone a few days and he agreed that it was a good idea to visit my sister and he thought it would do me good because I was looking tired. He thought it was to do with me putting on some weight and it would do me good to have a little break. Have I answered your question, Eleanor?'

'Yes, but I still think it strange that you have said so little about your time away. It is as if you have a secret to tell and I do not know how you got home so early in the morning. However, I am sorry to hear about Auntie Izzy and I do hope she gets well soon and copes better with her baby. I would like to go to Carlisle to see her and the baby.'

'No, No, No! You must not do that, Eleanor,' Muriel said hurriedly. 'She does not want visitors until she feels a lot better.' Goodness, thought Muriel, that would be disastrous. Izzy was bound to tell Eleanor all about delivering Muriel's baby. It was very convenient for her that Izzy was a midwife.

Her mother quickly changed the subject which did not go unnoticed by Eleanor.

'Now tell me more about your new young man, Eleanor.'

'Well I like him very much, Mother. I first saw him in the library and then I sort of bumped into him on the quayside and we walked along together to the Swing Bridge. He is a pupil of The Royal Grammar School and very interested in history. I have been telling him what I know of the history of Newcastle, which in fact is what both you and Father have told me at various times. We talk about other things as well and recently had a good discussion about education because Tom is going to college to train for teaching just as I have decided to do. We have a lot in common and enjoy one another's company.'

'You will have to bring him home for a meal, Eleanor, before he goes away. Your father and I would like to meet him.'

'I would love to do that, Mother. You will like him, I know you will but are you feeling up to having company? You have lost weight and seem a little preoccupied just now. Are you sure you are well? I am asking this for a reason because a few days ago I saw you sitting on the wall outside the workhouse on the West Road. I wondered whether you were feeling faint or breathless. It is quite a climb up to the workhouse.'

'No, my dear, I am fine. I was just waiting for someone I have got to know at St Matthew's church. I met her in one of the shops and she said if I had time could I wait for her and then go to her house for a cup of tea. I have to say I do not like being near that workhouse, it makes me shiver and brings back bad memories of the time your grandparents and my siblings and myself spent there.'

'Is that why you never talk about the Workhouse, Mother?'

'Yes,' Muriel replied. 'It is a part of my past that I want to forget.'

'Is there anything else in your life that you regret?' Eleanor asked.

'Not that I can remember,' Muriel replied. She was feeling rather uncomfortable now. Was that question deliberate she wondered.

Eleanor referred to the Workhouse again. 'The Workhouse makes me shiver when I pass it too, Mother. I just remember when that baby was left on the step of the Workhouse a few weeks ago. Wasn't that a dreadful thing to do?'

Muriel was feeling even more uncomfortable now. 'Yes it was a despicable thing to do; but when are you going to see Tom again?' she said, quickly changing the subject again.

'We are going to the Hancock Museum tomorrow. I have not been there since it opened six years ago, and Tom thinks it will be very interesting.'

When Tom and Eleanor met up the next day it was raining heavily as they ran sharing an umbrella to the museum from the city centre. They were very glad that they had chosen to be inside that day. They wanted to find out more about the museum and there was a steward there who was happy to oblige. He told them they were in for a treat as there were some excellent exhibits from around the world.

'The origins of the museum,' he said, 'could be traced back to about 1780 when a man called Marmaduke Tunstall began collecting ethnographic and natural history material from all over the world. After his death his collection was bought in 1791 by George Allan of Darlington. Then in 1792 when the Literary and Philosophical Society was founded in Newcastle its activities included the formation of a small museum and they acquired George Alan's collection in 1823. The National History Society of Northumberland, Durham and Newcastle upon Tyne was founded in 1829 and they used the museum for their meetings. The museum collections grew and grew until they were too big for the small museum and so they were moved to this site at Barras Bridge in 1884. The new museum was renamed the Hancock Museum in honour of John and Albany who were both local Victorian naturalists and who had helped to establish this new building for the collections. There is still a lot of work to do to make the building exactly how we want it for the collections which we hope to build up in the future. Our aim is to house collections which will be used by researchers from all over the world and I can see a time when students like yourselves in universities and colleges will find them valuable resources for their studies. It is very exciting and I would recommend that you come back many more times to appreciate all the work that is going to be done. It will be very informative and extremely interesting.

'Before you go, I must ask you if you have heard of one of Newcastle's most famous industrialists, Sir William Armstrong.'

'Of course we have,' Tom and Eleanor replied almost in chorus.

'Well it is he who is a major benefactor to this museum. He has given an enormous amount of money towards the construction of this museum and I think you will agree with me that it is going to be of enormous benefit to the people who live in Newcastle upon Tyne.'

'We will certainly be telling people about it,' Eleanor said.

'You look like two serious students,' the steward said, 'and I look forward to seeing more of you in the future. However, it is worth you having a look now at the beautiful display cases and cupboards and view the original collections which we were fortunate enough to obtain from the Literary and Philosophical Society premises.'

After thanking the steward, Tom and Eleanor thoroughly enjoyed an afternoon of viewing excellent displays of items from all over the world. It was a very informative and enjoyable afternoon.

On her way home Eleanor could not help thinking how well suited she and Tom were. They enjoyed one another's company in addition to having similar interests. He was a lovely friend and he had certainly helped during the last few weeks to relieve the anxiety she felt for her mother and how she was going to deal with her secret. Surely her mother would want someone to know what she had done in case there were any repercussions from her actions. She had tried her best the previous day, when she was talking to her mother, to get her to break her silence but she did not succeed.

Before they parted that afternoon Tom asked Eleanor to meet him on Sunday outside St. Mary's Cathedral. There was not time for her to ask why he had changed their usual meeting place but no doubt he would explain when they met up.

Chapter 13

A fter Robert's accident he became more and more disheartened and frustrated because he had no pay packet to hand over to Nelly. He was terrified of living in a Workhouse and the shame it would bring to the family.

His daughter Muriel seemed to understand the turmoil he was going through and to try and relieve his feeling of hopelessness she often took him for a short walk alongside the river. She knew how much he loved watching all the activity on the river and riverside. He had played his part in helping to build the big ships which were so much part of the river scene. It was very difficult for him now looking back at how fit he had once been. He very often fell into the trap of feeling sorry for himself and that did not help him at all. He always looked forward to the times when Muriel took him out for walks along the riverside. She did not seem to mind listening to all his woes and worries, particularly money worries.

The walks were very different from when he took her for walks when she was small. He had strode out then and Muriel's little legs could hardly keep up with him, but now his steps were awkward and unsteady and he had to have the support of Muriel's arm all the time. They quite often had to find somewhere to sit down so that he could rest the leg he had injured so badly in his accident, but Muriel had endless patience with him during his decline in health.

Nothing could be done about his failing finances and the Workhouse was looming ahead as a constant threat to their future. Robert's only comfort was the thought that people were not sent to the workhouse.

It was a voluntary decision and the workhouse was not a prison. Inmates could leave at any time after giving a brief period pf notice so that their own clothes could be retrieved and administrative formalities could be carried out. Families had to leave together, so that a man could not abandon his family to the care of the workhouse. Inmates could also, with permission, leave the workhouse to find work or any other means, by which they could support themselves. The older and more infirm people were unable to do this and probably would spend the rest of their lives in the workhouse.

One of the most unpopular aspects of entering a workhouse was the separation of inmates into different classes. Male and female, Infirm and able bodied, Boys and girls under 16, and children under 7. Some concessions were made for some contact between mothers and children but generally the different classes lived in separate sections of the workhouse building and had virtually no contact.

Robert knew from his working days when such things as workhouses were discussed at various times that in 1831 there were four parish workhouses in Newcastle upon Tyne. These were, St. Nicholas's, St. John's, St Andrews and All Saints', and were the same parishes who provided education in the 18th century.

In 1829 the Newcastle upon Tyne Board of Guardians decided to replace existing workhouses with a new purpose-built workhouse on a site to the west of the city at the top of Westgate Hill. The first workhouse buildings were erected at the junction of Westgate Road and Brighton Grove, and included an administrative block, a dining hall, laundry, bakehouse, workshops, school, sick wards, lying in wards, and an imbecile ward. Males were placed at the Western side of the workhouse and females at the East.

An infirmary was later built on to the workhouse for the inmates which was opened in 1840 by the Newcastle Poor Law Board of Guardians and as well as able bodied poor, accommodation was included for those suffering from illness or disability and for expectant mothers. In the end there were so many people in need of this kind of care, that a hospital was built on land close to the workhouse. Construction for this began in 1868 and it was officially opened on December 7th in 1870 by Thomas Ridley, chairman of the Board of Guardians. This hospital eventually became a major hospital called The Newcastle General Hospital, and it was in that hospital that James worked.

Unfortunately, Robert's fears were realised and the family had to go to the Workhouse but there was one good thing, in that by the time they were going to live there a children's ward had been added which meant the children were better looked after than before, but it was still a very dark troubled time for the family. It was torture for them all to be split up, and for the children, this was especially traumatic. They were separated from their parents and from Muriel, the sister they adored. Being older than her siblings she was put in a ward with older children and she fretted dreadfully about her younger brothers and sister.

For a long time the little ones cried themselves to sleep. They wanted Muriel to read or tell them one of her lovely stories before they went to sleep and could not understand what was happening to them. Where was Muriel? Where were their mam and dad? A funny lady with big black rimmed spectacles sitting on the end of her long nose, and black hair scraped back from her face, and horrible brown teeth, was looking after them, but she never smiled or gave them a cuddle before they lay down on their hard beds. She was horrid and even though they had not particularly liked school they wished over and over again that they could go back to St John's parish school again. Archie especially missed the word cards which were helping him to read. He had been getting so much better and his writing was getting so much neater but all learning stopped when he lived in the workhouse. He had to turn his thoughts to looking after his younger sister Izzy and his brothers, being the eldest of the siblings, but he hated it in the workhouse. He longed for Muriel to come but she had always told him to be brave whatever happened and that was what he was going to be. Muriel would have been so proud of him had she known how caring he was. He was just like a mini Muriel and helped the little ones brilliantly through such a traumatic time.

Muriel, of course, was broken hearted at being separated from her brothers and sister, whom she loved with all her heart. She worried about them constantly and tortured herself with thoughts of them. How would little Alfie manage in the mornings – he was always so sleepy and very slow at dressing himself and then there was Izzy who had such a nasty cough and who would calm her down when she coughed so much that it made her sick and frightened her when she thought she was choking. Then there was Tommy who refused to brush his hair and it was always sticking up and untidy and invariably covering his eyes This frequently led to tumbles and bruises. How would Donny manage if he was separated from the little wooden horse his father had carved specially for him and which went everywhere with him? Muriel's only comfort was the thought of Archie, who was such a good little brother and so kind to everyone and she knew he would be doing his best to look after his brothers and sister.

Fortunately, Robert's family were saved the trauma of seeing their distraught father's severe decline in health. He could not get over the fact that he could not provide for his family and he stressed so much about it that he had a fatal heart attack while in the workhouse.

That was the beginning of the end of their time in the workhouse. It was a miracle which saved them. One of Robert's mates at the shipyard, called Ronnie, had never forgotten his old friend. He admired his dedication to his family and his absolute integrity in all that he said and did. Robert had always said that his money was for his family and not for the profits of the Public House where his mates met for drunken revelry and gambling. Robert had also been extremely kind to Ronnie when he got himself into trouble with the police and had desperately needed a friend. It was because of Robert that he had managed to turn things around so that his life was now settled and he had a nice home and a good job again. He was enormously thankful to have had Robert as a friend.

Then in a stroke of unbelievable luck Ronnie was left a considerable amount of money by a distant relative and when he heard of his friend Robert's death he wanted to help his wife and family. He had secretly admired Nelly for years and this was a marvellous opportunity to help her. When Nelly found herself the recipient of such a large sum of money, she was able to take herself and all her children out of the workhouse and eventually live in a much better house in the Sandhill area. Ronnie visited them frequently and became a good friend of the family. He would have liked to take his friendship further with Nelly but although she was immensely grateful to Ronnie she did not want to marry him. It was a tremendous relief to be free of the workhouse, but Nelly grieved for her husband and the father of her children who now were such a comfort to her. Robert would be so pleased that they were all safe and happy again and she could imagine him thanking Ronnie over and over again.

Muriel too was very happy to leave the workhouse and be free again. Then to her great delight she met up again with her childhood friend Cyril Delaney. The old attraction between them was still there although Muriel could not bring herself to tell Cyril about her life in the workhouse. Her feelings were growing for him and when he asked her to marry him she was overjoyed. He was an intelligent man who had a good job and would be able to provide well for her. As her mother said on more than one occasion, 'You have done well for yourself, our Muriel, but it is no more than you deserve You will make a good wife for someone.'

Cyril was of that opinion too and they were married in 1842 and she left The Side for ever. She never again referred to her life in the workhouse, even to Cyril. It was a part of her life she wanted to forget. She felt a pang of guilt at not telling him but she could not lose Cyril because he was everything to her. She must never deceive him again. She meant it of course at the time, but no-one knows what lies ahead.

Chapter 14

Tom was waiting for Eleanor outside the cathedral when she went there on Sunday morning. He was not alone. Standing beside him were a lady and a gentleman very nicely dressed and to her relief smiling a welcome. She had already guessed that they must be Tom's parents before Tom introduced them. They were very well spoken and she hoped their warm greeting was sincere but strangely enough she did not warm to them as she had done to Tom. They were just holding back she thought, until they knew her better, although they did say very politely that they were pleased to meet her as a friend of their son.

Tom's father explained that they had been immediately attracted to the church when they came up to Newcastle from London by train on one occasion, when they knew they would be moving to Newcastle. The church was the first building that they saw on leaving the Central Station and as soon as they were settled in Newcastle they made enquiries about it. They had learnt some of its history from one of their neighbours who attended St Mary's Cathedral.

In 1838 the local Catholic people, whose number was steadily increasing in Newcastle, passed a resolution which said 'It behoves the Catholic body to endeavour to erect a large and handsome church that may be at the same time as being an honour to their religion, an ornament to the town and capable to afford seating for about 1200 people'. The construction of the church began in 1842 and the church was opened on the 21st of August 1844 as a church. It was consecrated as a cathedral on 21st of August 1850. The Catholic populous had wanted to build an impressive church which glorified their faith and they had certainly achieved that.

The architect commissioned to design the building was called Augustus Welby Pugin and interestingly he favoured the Gothic Revival Style of Architecture which is why the church is built in that style. The tower and steeple had to be added later because funds ran out but they too were designed by Pugin.

Tom's parents had been told to look out particularly for the East windows with their beautiful stained glass. Those windows had been designed by Pugin and made by a Newcastle glass painter William Wailes in 1844.

There was one other thing Tom's parents had been told which is not very well known. It relates to the Typhus epidemic in Newcastle. There is an underground crypt in the land surrounding the Church but it was sealed up and covered by grass in 1848. Two men are buried there, namely Bishop William Riddell and Father William Fletcher. These men had risked their lives knowingly and unselfishly visiting and caring for Typhus victims rather than staying in the safety of the cathedral buildings. They themselves died from the disease and were buried in the crypt. When Tom's mother heard about that she said she was reminded of the words in the Bible, 'Greater Love hath no man than this, that he lay down his life for his friends'.

As Eleanor sat with Tom and his parents waiting for the service to begin, she looked round admiringly at this beautiful church. The dedication and love of the Catholic people for their church, now a Cathedral, was very tangible and was absolutely their spiritual home. The service they were attending was inspiring and Eleanor found herself praying for guidance as to how to deal with the knowledge of her mother's wrong doing...

Tom's parents said a rather guarded goodbye to her when they left the church and Eleanor could not quite measure what they thought of her. They were nice people and she hoped they liked her. Tom thanked Eleanor for coming to the Cathedral service and he asked if he could meet up with her the next week beside Grey's Monument. He added that it would be good if Benjamin joined them because he had an idea to put to him and if he could come he needed to bring with him, the picture which he was doing for Tom if he had finished it. Then before rushing off to catch up with his parents, he gave Eleanor a quick hug and kiss, which brought a big smile to Eleanor's face. Tom really was so nice and the next week could not come soon enough for her.

In fact, everything would be wonderful if she did not have this ache in her heart for her mother and what she had done. She was so scared that there would be retribution following her mother's actions.

When she got home and asked Benjamin about meeting Tom next week he was delighted, saying he would make sure the painting was finished so that he could take it with him.

'I wonder what this is all about,' Benjamin could not resist asking.

'I do not know any more than you, but it will be something good, knowing Tom.'

Benjamin went off to find his picture, painted in water colour to show his sister.

'It is very good,' Eleanor said. 'You have captured the atmosphere of the quayside and all the ships and boats are beautifully depicted. I love all the detail you have included. The little figures of people all doing various tasks is so clever and it is the sort of painting that you see something different every time you look at it. I can feel myself there. Well done Benjamin. Tom will be delighted with it. Have you showed Mother yet? Remember she said she would like a picture of the river to hang on one of our drawing room walls? Go and find her now. I am sure she would like to see it before we take it to show Tom next week.'

Needless to say, Muriel loved the painting and repeated her request for Benjamin to do a similar painting for her, because the River Tyne was so special to her.

The next week Eleanor and Benjamin met Tom at Grey's monument. Tom pointed at the building immediately in front of the monument.

'You know what building that is, don't you, Benjamin?'

'Yes, it is the Central Exchange and I know that it is like a triangle in shape because it fronts onto three streets: Grainger Street, Market street and Grey Street; but I have never seen inside it.'

'No, I don't suppose you have because it was only constructed between 1834 and 1838 and was only officially opened as recently as 1839. It is rather a grand architectural building and was built as a commercial trading centre and a news reading facility. I have been talking to someone who knows a lot about it, and he said it was a very popular venue for people to meet and trade. You could subscribe to it and become a member, which made it rather elite and members considered it a privilege to be a part of the Central Arcade. My friend said that his grandfather had attended the opening ceremony in 1839 and he was allowed to go inside the building. He was so impressed with the interior. He had never seen anything so unique and so beautiful.

It was therefore a disaster when a fire in 1867 almost destroyed the building. It needed a great deal of restoration but there was no money to do this, which resulted in the Exchange and trading part of it and the reading room had to close, in 1869.

'Now Benjamin, this is the part which will interest you. I have found out that the building reopened as an Art Gallery in 1870 and there are 400 works of art on display. They are hoping to remodel the interior of the building next year to make more public rooms, with the aim of creating a centre for social and cultural activities. There will be Ladies' and Gentlemen's reading rooms on the first floor and a smoke and chess room, a billiard room, Art Gallery, meeting room and refreshment areas. In addition, there will be photography and art clubs and that is my reason for bringing you here today. After the refurbishment is done, Benjamin, you will be able to join the Art Club where you will meet likeminded people and benefit from talking to other artists. You need to progress and move forward with your art and I think this will be an ideal place for you to do that. It will be most beneficial for you. I have arranged for us to go into the building today and we are going to meet someone who might be interested in your painting of the River Tyne, because the gallery welcomes local artists.'

Tom, Eleanor and Benjamin made their way into the former Exchange Building where they did indeed meet the man in charge of the Art Gallery. Tom told Benjamin to show the man his painting.

'I can tell at first glance that this is a beautiful water colour painting of the River Tyne,' the man said. 'You have caught the spirit of your subject making it very atmospheric. I can almost feel myself walking into the painting. Your attention to detail is excellent and the colours you have used are exceptionally good and unconventional. Did you mix them yourself?'

'Yes I did. I love experimenting with colour,' Benjamin replied.

'Well young man you certainly have talent and I would like to see more of your work. I hope you will join the new Art Group which will be held here after the refurbishment. Would you be able to do that?'

'I certainly would,' said Benjamin, looking more animated that he had done for a long time.

'Right then, Benjamin, give me your address, I will send information to you and contact you again when the art gallery reopens.'

Benjamin was absolutely delighted at the outcome of the meeting with the manager and thanked Tom profusely for what he had done. Eleanor too was loud in her praise for what Tom had done for Benjamin. She liked him more and more. He was so kind.

It was much later in 1894, when Tom had finished his teacher training and was back in Newcastle, that his parents told him that a Concert Hall had been opened in the Exchange Building which was now called the 'Central Arcade' and they had bought tickets to take him to a concert there. Eleanor was still away at teacher training college at that time but Tom told her later that the acoustics were excellent and the concert was exceptionally good. He promised to take her to a concert there when she was home again after college.

Chapter 15

Time was passing and not long after their visit to the Central Arcade Tom would be going to Training College. Eleanor remembered her mother saying that Tom should join them one day for their evening meal, to meet her family. She asked her mother if that invitation still stood.

'Definitely,' Muriel replied and an evening was designated for the occasion. Her brothers were asked if they could be present and Frank and Harry agreed to come. James also agreed but it was dependent on whether he was free and not on call for the hospital. Benjamin of course wanted to be there because Tom was his hero since he had found the way forward for him and given him such encouragement. So it was that everyone including Tom sat down together for the evening meal a few weeks before Tom went to college. He charmed everyone with his good manners and relaxed style and he showed an interest in everyone. There were no awkward pauses and the conversation flowed freely.

Tom was pleased to meet Eleanor's older brothers and was particularly interested in Frank's involvement with what was called the Railway Age especially when the North East had such a large part in it. Frank explained that his love of trains had begun when his parents took his brothers and himself on an outing to the Central Station which had opened in 1850. Queen Victoria and her husband Albert had come up from London to perform the opening ceremony. It was at the time when Muriel and her family were living in the workhouse otherwise Muriel and her parents would certainly have been at that ceremony.

That is why she was quite excited when Cyril had suggested that they visit the Central Station one day with their own children, who were soon fascinated by it. Their father told them that the station was designed by the famous Newcastle architect John Dobson and had one very unique feature, which was the roof. John Dobson had a rather limited amount of land upon which to build the station. It was a triangular shape but with ingenuity he designed a curved roof to follow the train track which meant he had to take advantage of new technology and he used curved wrought iron ribs to support the roof. which had never been used in Britain before. Glass was also incorporated into the roof design. When the station was finished it was hailed as being one of the marvels of the Railway Age and the design was copied by other architects, even in other countries.

Frank liked everything about the station. He loved the hiss of the steam trains as they passed through the station heading for new destinations and the sheer grandeur of the big trains with their huge wheels, glossy paintwork and hissing funnels.

'What tales those engines could tell, Father,' he used to say. 'I have made up my mind. I want to have a career in trains.' He was absolutely enthralled with railways and trains.

After that Frank spent nearly all his Saturdays at the Central Station watching all the activity there and taking note of the train's arrivals and departures. He always asked Benjamin to accompany him because there were so many things he could sketch or paint, but Benjamin nearly always declined the offer, mainly because of the long walk to get there which he said made him breathless.

Tom wanted to know more about the Railway Age in the North East.

'Well you will remember I have referred to the development of railways previously and mentioned George Stephenson and his son Robert who had brilliant engineering skills, which led to their significant contribution to the history of trains and railways in this two great giants of railway engineering namely George Stephenson and his son Robert. They have transformed the pace and style of British life.

'They had very humble beginnings, but they rose to worldwide fame, despite George being illiterate in the early part of his life. The father and son had brilliant engineering skills which led to their significant contribution to the history of Trains and Railways in this century.'

'Tell me more about this family, Frank,' Tom said.

'George Stephenson was born at Wylam in 1781, the son of a colliery workman. From a young age he had to work and bring money home for his family and his work was mainly connected with coal mines. He worked hard and was reliable in whatever task he was given in the mines. At the age of 14 he became an assistant fireman at the pit and at the surprisingly young age of 17 he was put in charge of a new pumping engine at one of the pits. He was fascinated by machines and from being a boy had liked nothing better than taking something apart to see how it worked.

'In 1802 he married Frances Henderson when his ability was beginning to be recognised by men in higher positions. He was offered a job as brakesman at Willington Quay, by Robert Hawthorn who was at that time the most celebrated engine wright on Tyneside and his salary was increased considerably. He and Frances set up home in Willington Quay and it was there that their son Robert was born in October 1803, but in late 1804 he took the job of brakesman at the West Moor pit and moved his family to Killingworth. It was there that in July 1805 Frances gave birth to a baby girl who died three weeks later. Her own health went into decline and she died of consumption in May 1806, aged just 37. After this George went through a very hard time and even travelled away from Tyneside to find work, leaving his son Robert with a housekeeper. On his return he learnt that his housekeeper had married his younger brother and she was perfectly happy to continue looking after the little boy. Robert loved his Aunt Nelly, who was like a mother to him.'

Tom interrupted Frank to ask something.

'Frank, you are telling me about a man and his son, who were brilliant engineers and yet you have said that the father was illiterate during the early part of his life. It seems unbelievable?'

'I understand your question, Tom and here are the facts. George had no early education whatsoever and was still illiterate at 18 years of age but he did eventually learn to read and write, though with difficulty. His spelling and writing were never good and throughout his life his letters were written for him first by his son Robert and later by secretaries. It was said of him, Tom, that his brain totally lacked the capacity to store theoretical knowledge, even the simplest kind but in compensation he possessed remarkable powers of observation and great shrewdness and above all outstanding ability where anything mechanical was concerned. It was these gifts which carried him to fame. He was able, if presented with any engineering problem to find out the cause unerringly and correct it, even those problems which baffled people with much more theoretical knowledge than himself. His ability was said to be almost uncanny. Despite this he was always conscious of his lack of education and it comes as no surprise to learn that he was determined that his son Robert would be educated. He was sent to school in Long Benton from an early age and when he was 12 his father took him away from the village school and sent him as a day boy to a private school in Percy Street in Newcastle run by Dr Bruce for middle class children. George of course by this time in 1815 was earning a good wage and was being sought after as a first class mechanical engineer.

'He was placed in charge of all the machinery in the neighbouring collieries of the North East and went on to have more and more responsibilities which made him a very rich man.

'George was never a miner but he did so much for the coal mining industry. On his underground engineering work he was assisted by his son Robert. When Robert left school he was apprenticed to George's friend to learn engineering skills and many of those skills were needed in work underground. It was at Killingworth Colliery that George constructed his first steam locomotive in 1814 which ran on iron rails. In July of that year the locomotive was successfully tried out on the Killingworth Colliery Waggon Way. He went on to build 15 more steam locomotives at Killingworth, all of which made the transport of coal from the coalmines to the River Tyne much easier and faster.'

Tom interrupted Frank again. 'Are you saying, Frank, that the "Railway Age" which made George and his son so famous had its roots in coal mining?'

'Yes I am, Tom, because the coal that was dug up in the coal mines had to be transported from the coal mines to the river if it was to be exported and then from the river to the sea. Transport is the key factor. Horses were used down the mines at first to bring the coal from underground to the surface of the mine, but from there it could be a very long way to a river, not to mention the sea.

'It was George Stephenson who had a vision of there being some faster form of transport and a network of railways throughout the country.

'In 1819 he began directing the laying of a new railway for Hetton Colliery in County Durham and three of his locomotives were used for that. He then went on to plan and direct the building of the Stockton and Darlington Railway, which was the first public railway in the world to use steam locomotives. It opened in 1825.

'From there he went on to direct the building of the Liverpool to Manchester railway which became the world's first public Railway to carry passengers as well as other commodities. It opened in 1830 and was operated entirely by steam locomotives, one of which was the famous 'Rocket'. Robert his son supervised the construction of the railway because by now he was a brilliant locomotive engineer. He was also a designer of bridges too and the most famous of these is the High Level Bridge which I am sure you will have seen, Tom. It is a marvellous feat of engineering.

'Things had come a long way since the old waggon ways were in existence for the mines. Those waggons were first pulled by horses, all the way to the rivers on wooden rails, then on cast iron rails and finally by steam locomotives. What a difference this must have made, so much faster and easier, thanks to George Stephenson and his son.

'An example of the difference the railways made to transport is that   before there was rail transport it took the fastest stage coaches 37 hours to get from London to Newcastle with numerous horse changes along the way but in June 1844 a train could cover the distance in 9 and a half hours.'

'Frank, all this is very interesting and I think we need more time to discuss it. Did Robert reach the same level of fame as his father?'

'Yes indeed, Frank and he had the added advantage of having had an education. They say he developed a much more cultured speaking voice whereas his father never lost his 'Geordie' accent and at times his speech was incomprehensible. Undoubtedly this father and son were two great men, Tom, of whom the North East are immensely proud and yet neither are buried on Tyneside. George died in 1848 and is buried in Chesterfield in Derbyshire where he lived during his last years Robert died in 1859 and was laid to rest in Westminster Abbey.'

'Thank you for all that information, Frank. It was most interesting. It still amazes me that George, a largely uneducated man from such a humble beginning, could achieve such fame and greatness.'

At this point Eleanor broke into the discourse saying, 'Frank, you will have to meet up with Tom again and have a longer discussion about the Stephenson family because Mother and Father want to talk to Tom. I know you are busy with your degree, but you can arrange to meet somewhere.'

'I would like that, Frank,' Tom said and before going home that evening he and Frank arranged a time when they could meet up.

It had been a very pleasant evening and Tom got on very well with Eleanor's parents. They were very happy for the friendship to continue. Before Tom left that evening he arranged to meet Eleanor outside the library the next day.

Chapter 16

T he next morning Eleanor met Tom outside the library at the appointed time. She wondered why their meeting place had changed once again.

Tom explained, 'It is because we are going into the library this morning, Eleanor, to talk about, would you believe it, books but first I want to say how much I enjoyed spending time with your family last night and the meal was excellent. You are part of a really nice family. I was telling my parents all about the evening and told them I could not imagine a nicer family to meet.

'I will be going away soon so I thought we would meet up in one of the places we like best and through which we first met. Books are on my mind just now because I have been informed of certain books I need for college. Only four weeks to go now and I have been thinking how lucky we are to be living in the Victorian period when so many good books are being written and even if education is not so valued books certainly are. We are fortunate that access to libraries is free because originally libraries were limited to the wealthy people. It was only in 1850 that the Public Libraries Act enabled towns to use rates to build free public libraries.

We are lucky too that this century has produced some very good authors. Do you have a favourite author, Eleanor?'

'Yes I do, Tom and it is Charles Dickens. He creates wonderful characters in his books and I like the way he highlights certain issues I am thinking particularly of 'Oliver Twist' published in 1839 because it highlights the injustices of society and the plight of poor people and their families and you know how I feel about that. Dickens had known poverty as a child and shows great compassion in his writing for the poor, hungry and homeless. He is most commonly linked with the great city of London so I expect you know more about him than I do Tom.

'Throughout his career he immortalised London's dark streets and troubled inhabitants in his stories. He was a very clever man and another man who had humble beginnings. He was born into a working-class family and had an impoverished childhood. He never forgot the lessons that childhood had taught him and although he was best known as a novelist, he was also a tireless campaigning journalist. He wanted some things to change. He wanted sanitary reform, gender equality, more efficient hospitals, prison reforms and education for all. He looked at the roles that poverty and despair played in crime and how much a person's past can shape their future. The essence of almost all Dickens' writing was the belief that those with money need to take responsibility for those who are impoverished and that is my belief. What a remarkable man he was.'

Tom broke in to say, ' Did you know, Eleanor, that some of his novels are serialised in monthly magazines before being published in book form and that he gave public readings from his novels to packed audiences in this country and in the United States?'

'Yes, I did know that, Tom but here is something I do not think you will know. Charles Dickens visited Newcastle six times between 1852 and 1867. His first visit was while acting as a manager of a touring company and he even acted in two of the plays. The Old Assembly Rooms in Newcastle at the bottom of Westgate Road actually hosted the plays as it could hold 300 people, but apparently when Charles Dickens was making an appearance there were 600 people and somehow they managed to find places for all of them. That was an enormous fire risk but he was very popular and so for them it was worth the risk.'

Tom broke in here to say, 'I wish you and I could have been present at one of his readings or plays. I have heard that he could make his books come alive with his readings and the audiences and critics were spell bound.'

'Yes that is correct, Tom because in 1858 there was a report in the Newcastle Chronicle, founded in 1764, which said 'Mr Dickens unites uncommon dramatic power and expression and his readings have all the interest of a well acted play.'

'My parents would endorse that, Tom because they attended one of his reading engagements in 1861. The meeting was held in the Music Hall in Nelson Street in Newcastle and Charles Dickens gave readings from his novels David Copperfield, Nicholas Nickleby, and Little Dombey, adapted from the early chapters of Dombey and Son. Seats were very expensive although poorer people were allowed in the standing gallery for a penny. My father also told me that there was a quote from Charles Dickens in one of the newspapers of the time which said, "At Newcastle against heavy expenses I made more than 100 guineas profit. A finer audience there is not in England and I suppose them to be a specially earnest people for while they laugh till they shake the roof they have a very unusual sympathy with what is pathetic or passionate".'

'That is a superb quote, Eleanor. I think it is wonderful that he came to give his readings at Newcastle upon Tyne. I think Newcastle upon Tyne has so much of which to be proud. It has prestige and deserves much more recognition for all that it contributes to the world, in the form of pioneers, industrialists, inventions, entrepreneurs, art and culture and many other things. It is a leading city of our time.

'Have any other authors caught your attention, Eleanor?'

'Yes but I have not read any of their books yet. I am looking forward to reading books which the Bronte sisters, Charlotte, Anne and Emily have written in this century. I have heard that Emily's 'Wuthering Heights' is excellent so I must try to get hold of a copy. It will be something to read while you are away at college because I am going to miss you so much, Tom.'

'I will miss you, Eleanor, but we will still see one another when I am home for weekends and holidays, and in no time at all you will be starting college yourself. We will be able to write to one another because since the New Post office has opened in Newcastle, written communications are much more reliable.

'Now I have something for you and your brother Benjamin as a little present before I go away. Yours is a book called 'Alice in Wonderland' written by Lewis Carrol in 1865 and it is a very clever fantasy. It is different and I am sure you will like it as it is very well written. It may also be of use when you are teaching and would be even better if Benjamin could do some illustrations for it That is why I am giving him a copy of Treasure Island because that book too lends itself to ideas for illustrations The book was written by Robert Louis Stephenson in 1883. Illustrators are in demand now that we are entering a literary phase. It is worth Benjamin exploring that dimension of his artistic talent. I have also managed to get you a copy of 'Wuthering Heights' by Emily Bronte.

'Reading is gaining such popularity. Does your father get a newspaper, I wonder. My father and grandfather always read 'The Times' even though it is expensive and meant for the upper classes. My father of course always likes to identify with the upper classes. I must say that it is so much better now that newspapers are not taxed and do not have such harsh laws about their content. They have had a long struggle for press freedom but it has been worth it; the tax was removed as recently as 1855. Much cheaper newspapers are the result and since then newspapers have been rolling nonstop off the printing presses, though I do not get much time to read them as I am concentrating on the books I need for college. I do, however, manage sometimes to sneak a look at my father's 'Daily Telegraph'.

'Now, Eleanor,' said Tom standing up suddenly. 'Why don't we go and find ourselves something to eat. It will be our last time out before I go away.'

He took Eleanor's hand and they walked out of the library into a new phase of their lives. The past weeks had been so happy and Tom wanted their last evening together to be special so he led Eleanor past the bottom of Northumberland Street, crossing the road to Grey's monument and from there down to Grey Street to the Royal Turks Head Hotel, opposite the Theatre Royal. Eleanor was surprised because she was not expecting to be eating in one of the best hotels in Newcastle but it was typical of Tom that he would choose somewhere really nice for their last meal before he went off to college. It was a lovely hotel built in 1837 and the meal and service were excellent.

When Eleanor thanked Tom for the wonderful meal she had just eaten Tom said, 'Only the best for my best friend.' He was so nice, Eleanor thought yet again and they had had a wonderful evening together. They both knew instinctively that their relationship was going to lead to a definite commitment between them. The future looked good.

Eleanor was so grateful to Tom for providing a distraction from her troubles from the very first day she met him. One day she would talk about it with him, but he was quite prepared to wait until the time was right.

They had said their goodbyes on the way home when Tom had kissed and hugged her and she was glad her parents were in bed when she arrived home as she knew she would break down if they asked too many questions. It wasn't really goodbye, only au-revoir, but she would miss him.

Chapter 17

Eleanor missed Tom very much in the following weeks and realised how much she cared for him. One evening her brother Harry, who was home from college for a long weekend, suggested she went with him to visit his friend Phillip in Ravensworth Terrace, Summerhill which was a short walk from their home. Eleanor had always liked Phillip and there were no awkward moments as they talked to one another. Conversation flowed freely. Harry and his friend Phillip were both studying at the same college. It was the Marine Technical College at South Shields. They were both very interested in a naval career and were students at this college. It had been founded in 1861 by a trust created by Dr Thomas Winterbottom, a former Surgeon-General in Sierra Leone. The college was formerly based in Ocean Road in South Shields but it had moved to a purpose built building in 1869. It is one of the largest merchant navy training colleges in the United Kingdom and attracts students from as far away as India and Africa. Harry and Phillip both felt they had chosen a good college and they were working hard and making good progress. They had had to choose one course from the many which the college offered. Harry was studying mechanical and electrical engineering while Phillip had chosen marine subjects such as navigation and naval operations. They both wanted to travel and it was Harry's greatest wish to travel round the world and learn as much as he could about it. Phillip did not have so much enthusiasm for travelling but wanted to work on ships. Harry's love of the sea had begun when he had watched the big ships sailing down the River Tyne to the river mouth at Tynemouth and from there out on the open sea. This was what he wanted, to be an adventurer and an explorer and lead an exciting life.

Phillip was a quiet young man, very different from his enthusiastic friend and having met Eleanor several times thought how nice she was. They talked so much, and Phillip asked Eleanor to meet him the next day at the entrance to Leazes Park. This meeting led to further dates and Eleanor could see that Phillip was getting fond of her. She did not want to hurt him, but it did become necessary to tell him that she already had a boyfriend and they could only be good friends. it was such a relief when he accepted that.

It had not gone unnoticed by her mother that Eleanor was becoming very friendly with Phillip and she could not help thinking what a good match that would be. A son-in-law whose parents lived in Summerhill, a very good area of Newcastle. Muriel had decided that she could call herself middle class now that she lived in Summerhill and her mind raced ahead to the wedding her daughter would have. She must make sure that Cyril was putting money aside for the wedding because it would have to be a grand middle class affair but when she talked to Cyril that evening he was not in agreement.

'Muriel, I cannot understand why you worry about status all the time. Tom and Phillip are both very nice young men and should not be defined by class. We have both come from working class families and I am proud of my roots. I have worked hard all my life and that is why we can afford to live in Summerhill, but I do not consider myself any more important a person for living here. The important thing is, that whether you are working class or middle class you should live honestly and honourably and always treat other people as you would like to be treated yourself. That is the true worth of a person and Eleanor has made a very good choice in Tom for a boyfriend. He has the attributes that make him caring, loving and kind and obviously well respected. You only have to look at Eleanor when she is with him to know how happy she is, and her happiness is what matters to me. They have known one another for almost two years and I would be happy if they chose to be together for the rest of their lives. Philip is a very nice young man but she hardly knows him, so please stop trying to control her life.'

Cyril was annoyed with Muriel. She was too concerned about appearances and what people might think. There were more important things to think about as was obvious when Eleanor came in that night and wanted to talk about her future career.

'I have applied to St. Hild's Training College at Durham because I have finally decided that I want to be a teacher,' Eleanor told her parents. 'The college is for females only and is very near St Bede College where Tom is a student.'

'Are you sure you will not miss your family too much?' Muriel asked her.

'Mother, of course I will miss you all but I have to show some independence and make a worthwhile future for myself. You have educated me well by sending me to Dame Allan's School where I have been very happy and I thank you for that, but it is now time for me to take responsibility for my life. I have loved school and I want to go on playing a part in education in Newcastle. The recent Education Acts in 1870 and 1880 have made a big difference in schools and I want to teach in one of those schools after I have been trained to do so.'

In response Cyril replied, 'I think you will make a good teacher, Eleanor and I am so proud of your decision. I am glad too that Tom is going to be a teacher. He is a very nice young man and you obviously think a great deal of him and he of you. In fact, your mother and I would be very pleased if you and he were to marry one day.'

Muriel had a question: 'On a practical note, Eleanor, where are you going to stay in Durham through the week, because you said it is too far to commute daily?'

'If I do gain a place at St. Hild's,' Eleanor replied, 'Tom has asked if I can lodge where he is lodging with friends of his family. I will simply take his place and his friends are more than happy to let me do that, which is great.'

What Eleanor said next was said very deliberately as she was still trying to get her mother to talk about what she had done.

'My going away to unfamiliar surroundings is not as bad as going into the unfamiliar surroundings of a Workhouse. I still remember that day Father read out that newspaper cutting "Baby found on the Workhouse step". Who could ever do a thing like that?'

She now had the satisfaction of seeing tears start to roll down her mother's face. At last she was going to reveal the truth, but Cyril was looking concerned and said, 'Why are you crying, Muriel?'

The interruption meant that the moment of truth never happened. Her mother merely said, 'I must be getting a cold, Cyril. My nose and eyes are beginning to stream.'

Muriel had reached breaking point. It would have been so good if she could have confided in someone, but the moment was lost, and she left the room. Eleanor never managed to raise the subject with her mother again.

A few days later her father wanted a word with her. 'I am worried about your mother, Eleanor, because I do not think she is well just now. She is very restless at night and sometimes shouts out in her sleep. I feel that she has something on her mind that is disturbing her. I have asked her about it, but she just keeps saying she is fine. I do not think she has been herself since going to see her sister in Carlisle. I still do not fully understand why she had to go to see her and she has not told me. She is usually so honest in telling me about her comings and goings and yet she has never spoken about that visit to Carlisle. She must have prepared for the visit too because she had made enquires about the times of the trains to Carlisle from the Central Station. It was lucky for her that the Newcastle to Carlisle Railway was in place then.

'Eleanor, do you remember her reaction when I showed her that cutting in the newspaper about the abandoned baby on the step of the Workhouse. She turned white and I thought she was going to faint and she was very upset.

'Knowing how much she loves children and especially babies I just presumed she could not bear to hear about cruelty to children. Has she said anything at all to you, Eleanor?'

'Nothing at all,' Eleanor said truthfully. Her father could not know how much she wished her mother had talked to her.

'It will have to remain a mystery then but one day I am sure we will find out the truth about her strange behaviour.'

In an attempt to cheer up her mother Eleanor suggested they had a shopping day together in town. Muriel loved going into the Grainger Market in the middle of town and that is where they went first. She liked the history of it. It had been built on the site of a former nunnery of St Bartholomew and one of the entrances to the market is on the appropriately named Nun Street, which in turn leads back onto Grainger Street. Muriel found it a fascinating place because it was always busy and there was so much to see. She knew it had been designed by the famous architect John Dobson and was part of Richard Grainger's development of the city centre. It stood on the street which gave it its name 'Grainger Street' and it covered over 80,000 square feet making it the largest indoor market in the world at that time. Its large spanned glass roof was very impressive. Muriel and Eleanor enjoyed walking around the many stalls. It was said that there were two hundred and four shops in the market which would make it difficult to get round all of them. It was definitely a place to visit more than once if not numerous times.

The market was divided into two parts. The Eastern section was a meat market laid out in a series of aisles and the western section was a vegetable market also laid out in a number of aisles. The whole thing looked like a large open plan hall.

Muriel was fascinated by the lighting system of gas mantles with their chains hanging and she could not leave the market without visiting the Weigh House. The latter had originally been put there to weigh meat as it entered the market and farmers could be seen bringing whole pigs in to weigh them. When Muriel and Eleanor were there they were allowed to be weighed on the scales. Muriel was surprised to see that she had lost so much weight and remarked on this to Eleanor who replied that she had noticed her weight loss and said, 'Are you worrying about something, Mother, because that can make you lose weight.'

'No. What would I have to worry about?' Muriel said, although inwardly she was quaking. She was getting worse. Her 'lost' baby consumed her thoughts now. She needed to know if her baby was being well looked after and safe, but she had no way of knowing and the thought that her baby might be unhappy or suffering in any way was intolerable. Sometimes she could not sleep at night through worrying about her little girl and even Cyril had remarked about her sleeplessness. He had even suggested that she should visit the doctor, but she was not going to do that. She knew what was the matter with her and there was no way of putting it right.

Days like today were good because they helped to take her mind off her troubles, and it was lovely to spend time with her daughter who was always good company. She was now saying something to her about the Grainger Market.

'Mother, I am surprised that you did not come to the opening of the Grainger Market in 1835. They say there were great crowds here to witness it. I also heard that there were even two grand dinners held within the vegetable market to mark the occasion. One thing is sure, Mother, no-one can really miss an entrance into the market because there are fourteen entrances from the surrounding streets.'

'I have heard too,' said Muriel, 'that having the market here has been beneficial to trade for other businesses. Twelve Public Houses and a Music Hall have been built very near it and it was that Music Hall in the Bigg Market in which Charles Dickens appeared when he came to Newcastle in 1861 to give a selection of readings from his books. I have also heard that a new stall is being added to the market in 1895 bearing the name Marks and Spencer's Original Penny Bazaar. You might be away at college when that stall opens but we can come and see it on one of the Saturdays you are home.'

After their visit to the Weigh House, Muriel and Eleanor came out of the market onto Grainger Street and crossed over the road to Market Street where a draper's and fashion shop had been opened in 1838 by a businessman called Edward Muschamp Bainbridge and by 1849 this shop housed 23 separate departments making it what is believed to be the world's first general department store. It had 400 staff by 1887 and sold a vast range of goods. Muriel and Eleanor loved spending time there. Muriel also liked to spend time in the Bigg Market, which was a short walk from Bainbridge's.

Newcastle was a major commercial centre even in Medieval times and there were many markets where people could buy just about anything they needed. The area from Newgate Street right down to St Nicholas's church was known as market territory. After Newgate Street crossed Grainger Street the area was known as Bigg Market and actually consisted of three streets, known as Cloth Market, Middle Street and Groat

Market. Muriel knew the area well because her own mother Nelly used to bring her there when she was a young girl. It was she who had explained the names of the streets to her daughter. The Cloth Market was the most interesting for Muriel because it was where dealers brought and sold blankets and linens. Her mother Nelly was very interested in materials because she enjoyed sewing and used to delight in making dresses for her daughters Muriel and Izzy. Naturally she wanted the cheapest material because she could not afford high prices. Muriel loved it when her mother involved her in the choices of material. As well as looking at them, Muriel enjoyed feeling the materials and choosing the ones she liked best, especially if it was going to be used to make a dress for herself.

Newcastle's Music Hall, affectionately known as 'Balmbras', was also situated in the Cloth Market. It was slowly becoming famous for its variety shows but it had a mixed reputation and was known to be 'rowdy'. This made it out of bounds for Cyril and Muriel's family. Cyril particularly was very strict about bad language and bad behaviour. The name 'Bigg Market' took its name from a particular kind of Barley which was sold there. Bigg is a Scandinavian name for barley. The Bigg Market had another purpose. It was here where farmers came to hire farm labourers. The men had to stand and look straight ahead and stare. Muriel remembered one occasion when she was staring at one of the men he winked at her, making her feel embarrassed so much that she blushed enough for her mother to notice but fortunately she met someone she knew and nothing more was said about it. The farmers used to bring carrier carts to take their hired men home and could clearly be seen and heard ratting down the old Cloth Market. Despite them being old and rattily, Muriel told her mother that she would like a ride in one of the wooden carts, but she was never allowed. Nelly said that it was a good job the carts were noisy because they drowned out some of the very rude words the uncouth farmers were using.

The Groat Market, which was the road on the other side of Middle Street parallel to the Cloth Market, was established in 1743 and as expected was so called because groats and wheat were sold there Muriel wanted to know what groats actually are. Her mother told her that they were oats with the husks removed and so could not be used for grinding flour. Groat in Northumberland dialect simply means wheat. The Groat Market was Muriel's favourite because it had little shops up the side of it with all kinds of things on sale and her mother nearly always bought her a little present. Middle Street in the centre of the Cloth and Groat Markets became the site for the new Town Hall.

Chapter 18

M uriel had really enjoyed her daughter's company and their afternoon in town. She had found that the best way to forget her troubles was some sort of action or distraction. It had been nice to spend a whole day with her daughter and regain something of the closeness they had once shared. Something had changed since the day she had 'lost' her baby. She had thought she could put it all behind her, but she had been mistaken. She regretted what she had done bitterly and had jeopardised everything that she loved. They said time was a great healer but regrettably that was not so in her case and as time went on she was finding it more and more difficult to even act normally but she knew she had to keep going for her family's sake.

It would not be long now before Eleanor went to college and that was going to be even harder because Eleanor had never been away before. Meanwhile Tom came back from college having done extremely well on his course and he had made up his mind to see if his old school had a vacancy for a fully qualified teacher and to his great relief they had. He was due to start teaching at the Royal Grammar school at the beginning of the Autumn term.

It was Eleanor's turn to leave home for college. Her parents went with her on the train from the Central Station to help her to carry her cases and to see her safely to the house where she was going to lodge. Phillip, who had become a very dear friend, came to the station to say goodbye and wish her well. He had understood when Eleanor told him that she was committed to Tom but would always have a fondness for his friend's sister.

Eleanor could not help being a little apprehensive leaving home for the first time but it was exciting too, stepping out into the world. She looked upon it as an adventure. Tom was regrettably absent for the farewells because he was teaching now and could not be given a day off school, but they had said their goodbyes the evening before. Tom reassured Eleanor that she would be alright at St Hild's. He and Eleanor had viewed it from the outside but both presumed the inside of it would be similar to St Bede's college. The style of it was the same as St Bede and both colleges had a consecrated chapel in their grounds.

Tom had thoroughly enjoyed his time at college and Eleanor was right when she said the views over the River Wear and beyond were spectacular. He had, however, concentrated on his studies and was rewarded when, at the end of his time at St Bede, he was awarded a distinction in Education.

Eleanor was delighted for him. She had seen a good deal of him because true to his word he came home every weekend and they always met up somewhere to have a long walk and talk. Tom's parents had invited them both for a meal on one of those weekends and Eleanor had the feeling she was being tested for her suitability to be their beloved son's wife. She hoped they did not know about the workhouse experience. His parents would not like that. Tom agreed with Eleanor that she was being 'checked out' but it was a lovely evening and such a relief when Tom told her she had passed the test with flying colours. His parents liked her very much indeed and would be very happy if their friendship led to an engagement. Tom and Eleanor were delighted about that because Norah, his mother, was very hard to please.

Eleanor had visited Tom or he her regularly while he was at college and it was on one of those visits that they had made the decision to get married and it was a decision they shared with their delighted family but they did not get engaged immediately because Eleanor still had her teacher training to do.

They both loved the city of Durham and during those four years of training when one or other of them were training they had been able to explore the historic city of Durham. They stood in awe of Durham's magnificent Cathedral and the beautiful setting of the Palace Green surrounded by ancient buildings. They had loved the very old library in what had been the dormitory of monks who had lived there, in the past. It was so atmospheric and Eleanor, who was not very tall, was pleased to see that to reach the top shelves, someone had made a movable wooden platform accessed by rungs of a ladder. It was an intriguing structure but very safe and effective. The library had a wonderful collection of very ancient books which was very interesting for Tom and Eleanor, loving books as they did. They had walked through the cloisters and immerged into daylight and a cluster of buildings which also belonged to the Cathedral. From there they had walked down one of the very old streets leading to the River Wear and Prebends Bridge from where they could admire the beautiful views of the river. They had some lovely walks along the riverside, delighting in the views and woodland paths and enjoyed exploring the old streets and hidden walkways in the city itself. They never seemed to tire of one another's company and fell more and more in love. They became more and more sure that they wanted to be together forever. They were so pleased that both sets of parents hoped that they would stay together for ever. It was so obvious that they were very well suited.

Benjamin, who had especially missed Eleanor when she went away, surprised everyone. He had joined the Art Club at the Central Arcade and found himself painting pictures for quite a lot of people. His most popular painting was the one he had done for Tom of the Ships on the Tyne. Since joining the Art Club he had made some good friends, gained a lot of confidence and was much more sociable. He even confided in Eleanor that he had a new friend. Her name was Victoria and he liked her more each time he met her. This was good news for the family because Benjamin was much more confident and self assured. He also smiled a lot more because he was so happy.

In due course Eleanor qualified with a Distinction in Education just as Tom had done and came back home to live. She found out that Philip had met someone else shortly after she went away to college and they were now engaged to be married. Over the following weeks and months, Eleanor and Ella, Phillip's fiancée, became very good friends as did their husbands and the four of them frequently met up for meals or theatre visits. If Harry was free at any of those times he joined them with his girlfriend Kate. Sometimes Frank took time out from his studies to join them with his fiancé Edith. James' work at the hospital was so demanding that he hardly ever went out with them.

Whenever Ella and Eleanor met up for coffee they talked endlessly about Ella's forthcoming wedding. It was an exciting time and when Ella asked her to be a bridesmaid Eleanor was delighted. Phillip asked Harry to be his best man, which pleased Harry very much.

They had a wonderful wedding in the beautiful 13th century church of St John's at the foot of Westgate Hill on the corner of Grainger Street. After the service Tom and Eleanor went to look for a very interesting feature of the church. It had an anchorite cell attached to it. There was an opening in the wall in the form of a Greek Cross and behind that opening was the cell. When the cell was inhabited by an anchorite, a man who had withdrawn from the world for religious reasons, he could look through the hole and listen to the service.

During the marriage ceremony the light was streaming through the medieval stained glass window which is special to the church as it dates from 1400. The light from the window seemed to shine directly on Ella, making her look very ethereal and beautiful.

Tom only had eyes for Eleanor, the bridesmaid dressed in a beautiful shade of blue to match her eyes. Tom thought she looked stunning and he now put his plan into action.

At an appropriate moment after the service was over, he drew Eleanor aside, got down on one knee and asked Eleanor to marry him. When he took a tiny box containing a beautiful sapphire ring out of his pocket and slipped it on Eleanor's finger there was a loud cheer and a round of applause. Eleanor was thrilled and could hardly contain her emotion and great joy. Later they decided that their wedding would take place the next year when Eleanor would have completed one year of teaching and be well settled into the school to which she was appointed. This would give them plenty of time to plan the wedding. They decided to ask if they could get married in St Nicholas's Cathedral, where Eleanor's parents had been married in 1862. It was now a Cathedral because in 1882 the Diocese of Newcastle was created by Queen Victoria and the church became the Cathedral Church of St. Nicholas, the most northerly cathedral in England at that time. Newcastle was now a Cathedral City. St Nicholas' church had always been a very big Parish Church and was worthy of its new status.

To their great delight Tom and Eleanor were given permission for their marriage to be in the Cathedral and they could now begin confidently planning their wedding, for the following year. Eleanor was glad to find when she left college that Tom had settled very happily into his teaching job at the school which he had attended as a pupil before going to college, namely the Royal Grammar School. It was a very good school dating back to the 16th century when it was founded in 1525 by a man called Thomas Horsley who at one time was Mayor of London. Strangely enough the planning for a good grammar school in Newcastle had begun as early as 1477 but the building of the school was much later in 1525.

'Did you know, Tom, that your grammar school is the oldest institution of learning in this city?'

'Yes, I do know that, Eleanor,' Tom replied. 'I also know the school's motto, which is "Discendo Duces", meaning "Through Learning You Will Lead".

'I think that is very apt for you and I, Eleanor. When we first met, I asked you to tell me about the history of Newcastle and I have learnt so much from you. We both like learning, which in time has led us on to lead and teach children. We have learnt so much during our college years which is coming to fruition through our teaching. I have already found it very fulfilling and I am sure you will too.'

'I am going to remember the words of that motto, Tom. You are right They do epitomise us: "Through Learning You Will Lead".'

Tom interrupted her. 'That motto was something that all the boys who attended the Grammar School had to know by heart and they were reminded of it nearly every day. I know through being a pupil there. I found out something recently which provides a nice little link in our own history, Eleanor. In the early days of the grammar school being built, lessons took place in a building in St Nicholas's churchyard.'

Chapter 19

I t was not long after Phillip and Ella's wedding that Eleanor was appointed to St. Paul's School which was very near Summerhill where she lived. She was interested in its history because the building was very different to what you might expect a school to be and she did some research.

The school had opened in 1862 in a building called The Barber Surgeons' Hall, which was built by John Dobson, and was rather distinctive in style. In fact, it looked a little incongruous in the Elswick area of Newcastle but fitted well in the Summerhill area nearby. It was built for a very specific purpose and was one of three Barber's Halls to be built in Newcastle. The former halls were in the Manors Station area of Newcastle but had to be demolished for various reasons. The second Barber Surgeons' Hall in the Manors area was leased by the Durham University School of Medicine and Surgery which later became the School of Medicine in the King's College Division of the University of Durham. This second building was used by a Dr. Fife in 1829 to deliver his anatomical lectures to students. He was known to use the bodies of people who had been executed on the Town Moor. In one case the body of a young woman who had been executed was put on display in the Barber Surgeons Hall for people to come and see and apparently there was no shortage of people coming to see it. Thankfully the executions on the Town Moor came to an end in 1844 after the hanging of Mark Sherwood of Blandford Street who had killed his wife. This second Barber's Hall also came to an end when it was demolished in 1835 to make way for the Railway Viaduct to Manors Station, which is in the vicinity of the Central Station.

In 1851 John Dobson was asked to design a third Barber Surgeon's Hall in the Elswick area of Newcastle and he built it in Palladian Style. It is not known why the hall was built in Elswick. There is no other building like it there and certainly no other building with medical connections. The nearest medical building when it was built was the Workhouse on Westgate Road with its attached infirmary.

For some unknown reason the Barber Surgeons' Hall in Elswick had to be sold not long after it was built and the building was closed. closed. It did not re-open until 1863 when it became a school, known as the St. Paul's National School. It was to this school that Eleanor was appointed on leaving college, in 1896. Some changes had of course been made to the building to make it suitable for teaching purposes. Eleanor loved the imposing frontage of the building which remained intact after all the changes and also the old Latin motto which had been etched into the stonework above the entrance could still be seen. She had felt an affinity with the school as soon as she began to teach there and it was very convenient for her as her home was only at the most five minutes' walk away.

She loved the school and settled into her new surroundings very well indeed. She felt that she belonged in a classroom and looked forward to going into school every day. She had not forgotten of course that she and Tom were going to get married during her first year of teaching and there was a lot to discuss when she and Tom spent time together.

They were still very good friends with Phillip and Ella and often met up with them. Ella loved talking about Eleanor's forthcoming wedding, but one day she had something very exciting to tell her friend. She and Phillip were going to be parents. Tom and Eleanor were delighted for them..

It was wonderful news but their joy was short lived. Ella miscarried at three months and that unfortunately was the first of a number of miscarriages until Phillip and Ella were told that it was very unlikely that Ella would ever be able to carry a baby full term. In fact her life could be at risk because she had a condition which could cause severe haemorrhaging. Everyone was very disappointed for them but Phillip and Ella desperately wanted a baby and began looking into adoption.

Neither Phillip or Ella minded if their adopted child was not a baby and not long after their decision to adopt they were told about a little girl of seven who needed a new home. They were invited to go and see her which they did and fell in love with her immediately. She was such a pretty little girl with beautiful white blonde curly hair. She was perfect for them and they welcomed her into their lives. She very soon settled into her new surroundings and though Phillip and Ella were told very little about her background they loved her unconditionally. She was called Annabel and was a very lively, happy little girl.

There were one or two battles when her curly hair was being brushed out but she brought great joy to Ella and Phillip.

Phillip and Ella had a celebration tea for friends and family when Annabel came to live with them. Tom and Eleanor were invited and excited to see their friends' new daughter. The little girl skipped up to them and Eleanor's eyes immediately settled on her hair. It was a beautiful colour being white blonde, but it was the curls that were so distinctive. Annabel's curls were very tight and close to her head and Eleanor knew where she had seen curls like that. It was her very own mother Muriel. She could not believe what she was thinking. Another noticeable thing was Annabel's eyes. They were beautiful blue eyes like those of her mother Muriel, Benjamin and herself. Everyone commented on their blue eyes. Was it just a massive coincidence or was she looking at her little sister? It was a moment when the world seemed to stand still and Eleanor could not take her eyes off the little girl. She was gorgeous and Phillip told her later that she was very bright and could sing beautifully. That made three similarities with their family, hair, eyes, and singing voice. Could there really be a connection? Eleanor asked herself. She could not resist hugging Annabel as if she would never let her go. She would have to find out more about her, of course, but Eleanor had felt an immediate rapport with the little girl. She was also hugely relieved that if it was her mother's baby and therefore her sister, she had been very well loved and looked after.

It was very hard keeping what she thought to herself but she dare not talk about it to anyone, not even Tom. She wished now that she had told him the reason for her tears on that day when she was so distressed. It was much harder now to explain.

She could not share her thoughts with anyone because she had kept the secret for so long and it must remain a secret. Her own wedding would soon be here and she was worried about her mother's reaction when she saw Annabel at the wedding. Would she begin to ask questions and how was she going to answer them without revealing the truth. The past should stay buried in the past or more lives would be disrupted.

Eleanor's wedding day was approaching rapidly. Annabel and a college friend of Eleanor were going to be her bridesmaids and Ella her matron of honour. Eleanor was kept very busy with arrangements for the wedding and all her thoughts were centred on it so that she did not have time to worry about anything else. It was a good distraction. Muriel wanted to make her daughter's wedding dress and Ella, as matron of honour, was going to make her own dress and the other two bridesmaids dresses. They were to be a beautiful shade of pink which would look really lovely with Annabel's beautiful blonde curls. Eleanor was relieved that Annabel's mother was making hers and the bridesmaids' dresses because if Muriel had made the bridesmaids' dresses fittings could have been worrying if her mother was in the company of Ella and Annabel for very long. She might have asked some awkward questions.

Eleanor and her mother went to Newcastle to buy the material for her wedding dress but this time did not buy the material from the Cloth Market. They bought it at Bainbridges, their favourite department store because only the best was good enough for their precious only daughter. Muriel was very busy in the weeks leading up to the wedding and for her it was a welcome distraction because Eleanor's wedding had brought back memories of her other daughter, the one she had abandoned. She had tried and tried over the years to push what she had done to the back of her mind and put the past behind her but she had not been able to overcome her feeling of guilt and thoughts persisted of what life would have been like if she had kept her baby. It was now seven years since she had given birth to her sixth baby and she realised fully now the meaning of her mother's words when she had told her that you can run away from many things but you can never run away from yourself. Making the wedding dress helped to lift her spirits especially when she saw how beautiful Eleanor looked wearing it.

Eleanor was busy right up to the wedding day because there was so much preparation to be done for the wedding. One of the important things was to take Annabel to the cathedral to practise the special song she was going to sing at the wedding. The cathedral was very big and Annabel had never sung in such a big place and in front of such a big audience. She need not have worried because Annabel was very confident and her love of singing overcame any nerves she might have.

It was a relief when the Wedding day finally arrived. Everything had been planned very carefully with great attention to detail and it all came to fruition on the day when everything went very smoothly and Tom and Eleanor could relax and enjoy every moment of it. The weather was glorious and everything looked at its best. All Eleanor's brothers looked extremely smart and handsome and she herself looked absolutely stunning. Her dress was beautiful as were those of the bridesmaids. All the dresses had hand sewn tiny crystals on the bodice which shimmered and sparkled as they caught the light and made the Bride and all her attendants look absolutely beautiful. Cyril and

Muriel looking around at their family that day were immensely proud of them all.

The smallest bridesmaid had caught Muriel's eye immediately. She was gorgeous with her white blonde tight curls and beautiful blue eyes. When she sang tears filled Muriel's eyes. She had a beautiful voice for one so young and reminded Muriel of herself at that age when she loved to sing and perform in front of an audience. An unbidden thought entered Muriel's head. Could this child be related in any way? There were some similarities, beautiful blue eyes: white blonde very curly hair and a beautiful singing voice like herself. Then came the realisation that Annabel could be her very own child. At that precise moment Cyril turned to speak to Muriel and saw that her face had drained of colour and she looked as if she was going to faint. He gently lowered her down onto her seat.

'Whatever is the matter, Muriel? You look unwell,' Cyril said softly.

'I am alright, Cyril. Please do not fuss I am feeling better now.'

The truth was she did not feel any better. All her anxieties and fears had come flooding back. What if Annabel was her own child? Her child would be seven now and she knew that Annabel had been adopted so it could be a possibility.

Muriel managed to keep her composure until the end of the service, convincing herself that she was being very fanciful. Cyril bent down to take her hand and help her to her feet to sing the last hymn. She kept her composure throughout the meal and speeches after the ceremony but Cyril was worried about her. She was not her usual gregarious, lively self and instead of smiling and welcoming their guests she looked apprehensive and miserable. Cyril could see that she was finding it difficult to socialise on this special day. Normally she loved such occasions and it was obvious something was the matter. He was glad when it was time for them to leave and he could take Muriel home. She wanted to go straight to bed so he had no time to talk to her. They were both tired and no doubt Cyril thought, she would talk about what was troubling her in the morning. Cyril did not go to sleep immediately because there were some things that were puzzling him concerning Muriel's behaviour.

Muriel could not sleep at all. She found herself forced to look back which was something she had not allowed herself to do for a very long time.

It had been a great shock seeing Annabel at the wedding and seeing her resemblance to their family. She would have to find out somehow if her suspicions were correct. What if the child was her daughter? What could she do about it? Her mind was racing. She had thought she was free of the past and now almost seven years later it had caught up with her. She had thought it all out so carefully at the time and her plan had worked until now. Had the moment of truth finally arrived?

Why she did what she did was still a mystery to her. She had lived a fairly ordinary life and she was content with it. She had a husband and five intelligent children, all of whom she loved dearly and she would never want that to change. Her family were always demonstrative in showing their love for her and there was a trust between them all which had built up over many years. She had taught her children to treat other people as they themselves would like to be treated and they had grown up to be thoughtful, caring young people. So why had she let something happen which could destroy that trust and put everyone's happiness at risk?

It had been a tremendous shock to find out that she was pregnant again at 50 years of age. She had not expected that at all and she was terrified. She did not want another baby. Eleanor was 17 now and the boys would be so embarrassed. Life was so good at the moment. She had managed to get some part time secretarial work at the school where Eleanor was teaching and was enjoying the freedom of not being tied to household tasks and bringing up young children. She had had such a bad pregnancy with Eleanor and she and her husband Cyril had agreed that there would be no more babies. Childbirth held many risks and at 50 years of age the risks would be greater. A baby was the very last thing she wanted at this time in her life and she was sure Cyril would not take the news very well because on his own admission he was not good with babies. He was very much in agreeance with Muriel that Eleanor was to be their last child. One thing she was sure about was that she would not abort the baby because in her eyes that was morally very wrong but she had to do something. She decided not to tell Cyril or any one of her family..

Fortunately, she did not have morning sickness and did not put on too much weight. The weight she did put on she laughed off as middle age spread and she wrote to her sister in Carlisle asking if she could come to stay for a few days in November which was the month when the baby was due. She told her sister not to mention that she was coming to see her to her family and that she would explain when she saw her.

A few months after that one day in November Muriel set off for the Central Station carrying a large bag containing all the things you need for a new baby and she boarded the train for Carlisle. She had previously checked that the train was running because the Newcastle to Carlisle Railway was one of the newest rail tracks in the North East and one of the first trains to carry passengers.

She reached her sister's home in Carlisle safely and two days later her sister delivered Muriel's baby, a beautiful baby girl. Muriel held her new daughter in her arms and had to fight with her inner self not to bond with her. She loved babies but she had to harden her heart, no matter how difficult that was. She could not help loving her of course and she always would. She wished with all her heart that she could keep her but it was too late for regrets. She could not go back on her plan. She was very surprised and very thankful that everything had gone so well and she stayed with her sister a further few days before being offered a lift to Newcastle by her sister's son-in-law, travelling in his pony and trap. He was coming to Newcastle on business and was glad of the company. It was not quite the transport Eleanor would have wanted but she wrapped the baby up warmly with the shawl she had knitted so lovingly for her first baby and all those who followed. She had kept it safely wrapped up at home after Eleanor her last baby, was born and did not really want to part with it but giving it to her new baby would make a connection between them. It was such a poignant moment when her baby was born. She had tried to remain detached throughout the pregnancy but had forgotten that wonderful wave of love and feeling of protection which accompanies childbirth.

It was not a very comfortable ride in the pony and trap but Muriel managed to feed the baby on the way home, so that she would not get too hungry if she was not found immediately. They had to make an early start as there was some distance to Newcastle from Carlisle but they arrived safely in Newcastle and Eleanor told William to put her off at the new hospital they were building on the West Road next to the workhouse. She told William that she was going to get the baby checked over at the Workhouse hospital.

It was very early in the morning and still dark, and as an extra bonus rather misty, all of which somehow made it easier to do what she had to do. She hugged the baby to her and whispered I am so sorry, I love you so much and then she laid the baby on the step of the entrance to the Workhouse and crept away without a backward glance. If she had looked back she knew she would have changed her mind. Her heart was breaking.

Daylight was just dawning when Muriel made her way down Westgate Hill to her home in Summerhill. She was sure that no-one had seen her and was totally unaware that someone was observing her from a distance.

That very morning Eleanor and Benjamin were out and about very early. Benjamin had persuaded Eleanor to get up and go with him to see the sunrise over a part of the Town Moor called Nun's Moor which was only a short walk away. He wanted to paint the sunrise when he came home but did not want to go on his own and so Eleanor had offered to accompany him.

The sunrise was magnificent and Benjamin was in a hurry to get home so that he could begin his painting. They were on their way home down the West Road and were about to pass the Workhouse when Benjamin set off running ahead of her, shouting over his shoulder that he was getting in some running practice. Eleanor remembered him saying that he was trying to lose some weight and in addition trying to improve his general health. He was determined not to let his weak chest dominate his life and every day he tested himself by running a little bit further. It was all downhill now to Summerhill and so it was a good time to do some practice. It was good that he had gone ahead because he did not see what Eleanor was just about to witness. It made Eleanor stop abruptly. A woman was approaching the door of the workhouse and it looked as if she had a baby in her arms. What happened next was unbelievable. The woman was wrapping a shawl more tightly around the baby before laying the baby on the step of the workhouse. Surely the woman was not going to abandon her baby. Eleanor watched in horror as the woman walked quickly away. Eleanor was about to step forward and confront the woman when she turned slightly and Eleanor made the horrifying discovery that the woman was her very own mother. She suddenly felt quite faint and her instinct was to run after her mother but she was nowhere to be seen, having almost run down the West Road to Summerhill. Her instinct now was to look after the baby whose safety was paramount. She moved her position until she had a good view of the Workhouse and from where she could see the front step of the building. She did not dare take the baby herself but she was there to protect it if it was in any danger. To her immense relief someone did come to the door and there was a sharp intake of breath and a loud exclamation when she saw the baby but she lifted the baby up and took it inside with her. The baby was safe.

Eleanor started to run after her mother although she knew she would be well down the West Road and she could not catch up with her. There was no sign of her mother when she reached home, and Benjamin had obviously gone straight back to bed. He would have been ahead of his mother so he would not know anything. Eleanor went slowly up the stairs to bed. She wondered what reason her mother would give her father for coming home so early in the morning and would she tell him about the baby she had so cruelly abandoned on a doorstep. Her mother must give an explanation. Meantime she decided not to say anything at all about what she had seen. Sometime very soon she must have a very serious talk with her mother but for now she would try to get some sleep.

The next morning at breakfast Eleanor was sure her mother or father would say something about Muriel being out so early in the morning but neither of them said anything. Eleanor was so upset by what she had witnessed that she did not want to be in the same room as her mother and so she ran out of the house all the way down to the quayside and that is why she was walking with her head down beside the river on the morning she met Tom.

Two days after he met Tom her father read out a headline from the Newcastle Chronicle paper, 'Baby girl left on Workhouse front step' and he commented, 'Who would do a thing like that. It is a wicked.' Muriel replied to this by saying, 'There has to be something the matter with a person who would do that. I do hope the baby is looked after.' Eleanor could not believe that her mother was not explaining everything and she longed to ask questions about what she had seen but something was holding her back. It would be her word only and she doubted if her father would believe her anyway. It was so unbelievable what her mother had done.'

'How can my mother live with herself?' Eleanor thought.

'I am sure someone will take care of the baby, my dear,' Cyril said. 'It is not your problem so do not worry about it.'

Eleanor wondered what he would do If he knew the truth, but she knew that it was impossible for her to tell him. The truth would have to come from her mother.

Chapter 20

M uriel could not get any rest that night after the wedding. Every time she closed her eyes she saw that beautiful little bridesmaid Annabel. She would have to see her again and find out more about her background. How she was going to do that she did not know but it had to be done. She had spoken briefly to Ella, the child's mother and admired her little daughter. Ella's reply revealed another interesting similarity with Muriel's family.

'We are so thrilled with her, Muriel but there is something we have been told about her health which rather disturbs us. She has a weak chest and has asthma attacks.'

'Do not worry too much about that,' Muriel had replied. 'I had asthma as a little girl but have been fine for years and years.' This was true but was it just another coincidence.

It was no wonder that Muriel could not sleep as so many thoughts were going round and round in her head. What if Annabel did turn out to be her own child? What would she do? She could not acknowledge her as her own. That would be a disaster for the family and yet she did not think she could live near her without sometime breaking down. It would be torture to keep the secret but she could not under any circumstances reveal the truth. She had to carry on and continue to bear the heartache. Her past had certainly caught up with her. She was fighting tears when she finally fell into an uneasy sleep.

Meanwhile Cyril was also finding it difficult to sleep because certain things were bothering him. In fact, certain things had bothered him for some time. He was not asleep when Muriel had returned home so early that day four years ago. He had pretended to be asleep but he knew she was there because she was weeping ever so quietly. The next morning he had thought she would tell him all about her visit to Carlisle and the reason for her tears and early morning return, but she said nothing. He wondered why because they had a good relationship and had always talked things over together...

Another puzzling thing had been her reaction when he had read out the newspaper headline a few days after her return. She had seemed very upset about that. Yesterday in church she became very upset about something but why did she not tell him?. He must talk to Muriel tomorrow. He fell asleep on that thought.

The morning after the wedding when Cyril and Muriel came downstairs they felt very fragile, not having slept much with all their disturbing thoughts.

Cyril said very quietly, 'Muriel are you going to talk to me about what is upsetting you because I am sure something is the matter.'

'I do not know what you mean, Cyril,' Muriel answered. 'I am fine.'

'You are not fine, Muriel and I only want to help you.'

'Stop! Stop, stop, Cyril,' Muriel shouted, her voice rising hysterically. 'I keep on telling you I am fine but you just go on and on asking me. What am I going to do?'

'What do you mean, Muriel? What is troubling you? Please tell me.'

I cannot tell you, I really can't,' and again her voice rose until she was screaming, 'Go away. Go away' repeatedly. Her face turned red and streams of tears fell down her face and she staggered around the room coughing and spluttering.

Cyril was horrified to see her like this. She was working herself up into a frenzy which was not good for her and then his worst fear was realised when her breathing became erratic and she was getting more and more distressed. He had seen the signs before and it was not long before she was in the middle of a severe asthma attack. She was now gasping. 'Help me, Cyril. Help me. I cannot breathe.' But even before he could reach her side she fell to the floor and was beyond his or anyone else's help. He could not believe what had happened and was in such a state of shock. The wife he loved so dearly, Eleanor Muriel was dead, and he would now never know what was troubling her. Her secret had died with her.

Everything that happened after that was just unreal for Cyril. His safe happy little world was destroyed. His sons took over from their father and looked after all that had to be done, even though they too were in shock over what had happened. They knew their mother had asthma, but she had never had an attack for a very long time. Something must have triggered it, but they had no idea what that could be.

The worst thing they had to do in the aftermath was contact Eleanor who was of course on her honeymoon. Rather to their surprise she dealt very calmly with the news. It was almost as if she was relieved but of course they rejected that idea. They were not to know that Eleanor had been worrying about her mother and wondering how she had reacted on meeting Annabel. She had not shown her feelings at the wedding but was bound to have reacted in some way in the following days. The news of her death was shocking and Eleanor grieved bitterly for her but a part of her was angry too because her secret would have to remain a secret for ever somehow she resented her mother leaving her with it. She was, however, glad that her father was spared the anguish of knowing he had another child and her brothers too never found out or guessed that Annabel was their sister. The secret of her mother's wrongdoing was absolutely safe with her. She would see to that.

Strangely enough while on their honeymoon Tom had mentioned the first time they met and he asked if she was going to tell him now that they were married, why she was so upset.

'Tom I was just feeling hurt because my mother had gone away without telling me, to see her sister in Carlisle and she had previously said that I could go with her to see the new baby. It seems very trivial now but it was important to me at the time.' Eleanor was quite aware that she was not being truthful but to tell the truth would not benefit anyone and it would have to stay buried in the past.

There is always a mixture of emotions at funerals and Muriel's funeral was no exception. The suddenness of Muriel's death had shocked everyone and it was the content of much conversation and discussion in the weeks following. There was also a great deal of speculation. Most people were sympathetic, particularly so soon after her daughter's wedding. She had not shown any signs of illness in the weeks leading up to the wedding, although someone commented that they had seen her sit down suddenly in the wedding service as if she was not well and another said she had seen Muriel quite a few times sitting on the wall outside where the old workhouse had been. She looked as if she had been crying so perhaps she was not feeling well. A local shop keeper said that Muriel was always breathless when she came into his shop as if she had heart trouble and so the speculation went on. Cyril of course was heartbroken and could not help feeling guilty that he had been going to question Muriel about one or two little things that had mystified and worried him for some time. He had been briefly suspicious of her actions once but he now dismissed that suspicion. He had loved her dearly and he always would.

Two Eleanors in his life, his wife Eleanor Muriel and his daughter Eleanor. They each had the same secret, but he was spared from the truth. One Eleanor had died and the other was extremely good at keeping secrets and so no-one was going to be hurt in the years to come.

Annabel loved her new aunties and uncles and they were a big part of her life. She loved spending time with Benjamin because she liked drawing and colouring and Uncle Benjamin was so good at these things. He was helping her to improve her drawing and painting and she always liked learning new things. If she ever had a brother she would want him to be like Benjamin. She liked his girlfriend, Victoria, too. One of her favourite outings with Auntie Eleanor and Uncle Tom was to the library in Newcastle because she loved books. Auntie Eleanor had such a lovely book called 'Alice in Wonderland' and she loved sitting on Auntie Eleanor's knee while she read it to her. Annabel was learning to read of course at school and was looking forward to being able to read all her books herself. Another favourite outing with Auntie Eleanor and Uncle Tom was to the River Tyne, to watch all the ships and boats that were sailing on the river. They always took her to stand on or beside the Swing Bridge and told her about that being their favourite meeting place and where they had first met.

'Grandad Cyril', as she liked to call him was very special to Annabel. She loved her other grandparents too but 'Grandad Cyril' lived very near and she saw him almost every day. She called him Grandad because he was old and somehow very special. He looked after her like a second daddy and gave her so many lovely big hugs. Sometimes she thought he was never going to let her go. He told her once that she reminded him so much of his wife Muriel who had died.

When she started school at St. Paul's, he was always there to meet her when she came out of school in the afternoon and he was always interested in hearing what she had been doing that day. He also loved to hear her sing because he said that she sang like an angel just like his beloved wife Muriel. Auntie Eleanor was her teacher at St. Paul's School when she was in the first class and she looked after her just like a big sister. It was a pity Eleanor's mummy Muriel had died because she would have liked to ask her if she used to cry like she did when her hair was being brushed. She just might have known the secret of brushing out curls without it hurting so much.

On the other hand secrets were not always a good thing and she said to herself that she would never keep a secret, except at birthday times when you bought something for someone for a surprise and kept it secret until their birthday. That sort of secret could never hurt anyone. It was Benjamin's birthday soon and she had a lovely surprise for his birthday which she was not going to tell anyone about. It was Annabel's secret! BUT–

Reader, if you promise not to tell anyone, Annabel had another secret which was very special. Auntie Eleanor had told her that she was going to have a baby in a few months' time and that Annabel could be like an auntie and help to look after the baby. That was the best secret of all, and just like her Auntie Eleanor she would be the very best auntie that she could possibly be.